LIGHTNING WINGMAN

By

Thomas Willard

Approximately 35,000 words,

Copyright ©, Thomas Edward Willard, 2021.
All rights reserved.

PREFACE

As a twelve-year-old kid growing up in Lynn, Massachusetts - where General Electric's River Works jet engine division was the city's chief employer - I was obsessed with anything to do with airplanes.

My favorite television program was "Twelve O'clock High," loosely based on the 1949 movie of the same name starring Gregory Peck.

Though I didn't know it then, two of my paternal uncles had been pilots in the US Air Force: one, my namesake, flew during WWII, was injured in a crash, and eventually died from his wounds, and the other fought in the Korean War.

Coming from a blue-collar family – most of my male relatives were electricians - after high school, I went to East Coast Aero Tech (ECAT) at Hanscom Field in Bedford, Massachusetts, to become an aircraft mechanic, receiving both Airframe and Powerplant licenses from the FAA.

Thomas Willard © 2021

I graduated from ECAT in April 1971, at the height of the Vietnam War, when the draft was still in effect. My selection number was very low, so I enlisted in the Air Force that August rather than waiting to be drafted into the Army.

With both FAA licenses, I expected to be sent to Vietnam immediately after boot camp. However, after taking an aptitude test that showed I knew the electrical symbols for a battery and a light switch, I was considered an electronics genius and sent to a nine-month electronics technician school at Lowry AFB in Denver, Colorado, to study electronic instrumentation and telemetry.

After completing the training, I was stationed at Vandenburg AFB in Lompoc, California, assigned to the Air Force Systems Command, 6596 Instrumentation Squadron's satellite tracking station.

There, I joined a group of enlisted men attending Cal Poly in San Luis Obispo part-time and began studying for a bachelor's degree in mechanical engineering.

Thomas Willard © 2021

After my enlistment was up, I continued at Cal Poly for another year - until my money ran out - before returning home to complete my undergraduate degree at Northeastern University in Boston.

But while still at Cal Poly, I worked as a co-op student for three months at Rockwell International, formerly North American Aviation, at their facility in Inglewood, California, on the B1 bomber program.

The Engineering Section there was massive, all housed in one open bay suspended on a false ceiling of an old WWII-era hanger, with the gray tanker steel desks of the over 2000 engineers working there backed up one against the other.

I worked in the Stress Analysis Group, shuttling decks of punched cards used as input to the finite element analysis software to and from the computer room for the stress analysis engineers.

Though the work was tedious, my manager was very interested in developing his co-op students and would meet with us late every Friday afternoon to answer any questions we had.

Thomas Willard © 2021

With thousands of engineers, each working on the minutiae of the design – one engineer's job was to track the number and location of all the rivets to determine their effect on the bomber's center of gravity – I asked my manager who had come up with the concept for the B1, whose unique design features included a variable swept wing? The manager said to hold that thought and that he'd get back to me soon.

Good to his word, the manager brought a guest to the following Friday's meeting: Sam Iacobellis, the lead engineer on the B1 bomber program.

Iacobellis described a meeting the company had held at the Inglewood facility thirteen years earlier when he and eight other engineers sketched out the B1 bomber concept on a blackboard.

Then, after Iacobellis completed his brief description of the genesis of the B1 bomber, he listed some of the other famous aircraft the company had produced, including the Space Shuttle.

I was especially enthralled when he touched on the development of two of the company's earliest productions: the P-

51 Mustang and the F-86 Sabrejet, both designed and built in the same Inglewood facility we worked in.

After transferring to Northeastern University, to satisfy that school's one semester of co-op experience requirement to graduate, I worked for Raytheon Missile Systems Division at Hanscom Field in Bedford, Massachusetts. After graduation, they hired me to work on their Patriot missile system program.

There, I was accepted into a special graduate student program Raytheon had with MIT and eventually received a master's degree.

Like all the other recent college graduates Raytheon had hired to support the program, I was laid off when Raytheon lost the AMRAAM air-to-air missile contract to Hughes Aircraft.

But, after working for several other defense contractors in the metro-Boston area, I eventually ended up working back at Hanscom Field again, this time for the Department of Defense's Lincoln Laboratories, working on the design of a large parabolic antenna and its imaging radar system.

Throughout my travels, though, I never lost my interest in aircraft, especially in the two iconic WWII-era propeller-driven fighters, the P-38 Lightning and the P-51 Mustang, and the Korean-era F-86 Sabrejet.

The idea for the Wingman series began in the early 1990s when I became curious whether any US pilots had flown all three of the iconic fighters in battle.

I learned that many of the F-86 Sabrejet pilots who fought in Korea were WWII veterans, and most of those had initially flown either the P-47 Thunderbolt or the P-38 Lightning before transitioning to the P-51 later in WWII.

At about the same time, I'd heard a rumor of a rescue by a P-38 fighter pilot of another pilot during WWII.

I wrote to the Smithsonian Air and Space Museum in Washington, D.C., to ask if the rumor was true, and they confirmed that it was and that there was only one known successful rescue mission by a P-38 pilot. That rescue was well known in the P-38 pilot community, and the Smithsonian sent me the details of the rescue.

The pilot who flew the mission had just turned twenty-years-old that day. Though he was promoted from sergeant pilot to first lieutenant on-the-spot when he landed, he refused the Congressional Medal of Honor, saying he had only acted as any wingman would have during the rescue and wanted no special recognition.

In 2002, PBS presented an episode of the WWII detective series "Foyle's War," which featured an unrequited love affair between two Spitfire pilots who fought during the Battle of Britain. That raised another question: did any fighter pilots who fought in WWII later self-identify as gay?

In a search on the internet, I found several autobiographical books written by British and US pilots who fought in WWII and later divulged that they were gay.

Though there was a brief period of tolerance in the military during WWII, the pilots who fought in the war still had to be discreet and keep their gender preferences hidden.

One book, "Arise to Conquer," written by a hero of the Battle of Britain, Spitfire pilot Ian Gleed, required rewriting by Gleed to switch some male pronouns to female and to include a fictitious girlfriend named Pam before the publisher would agree to print it.

Gleed was promoted to Wing Commander in 1941 but was later shot down and died in a crash during the Battle of Tunisia in North Africa in 1943.

In early January 2021, like most contract engineers, I was laid off during Covid-19.

A year earlier, I had read about self-publishing on Amazon, and to occupy myself, I began writing the first book in the Wingman series, "Lightning Wingman."

In researching combat fatigue for the book, I stumbled onto the seminal work done early in WWII by psychiatrist Dr. John

Spiegel, which led to the USAAF Eighth Air Force's creation of rest homes for fatigued airmen, affectionately known by them as Flak Houses.

I also discovered that Spiegel, 30 years later, as President of the American Psychiatric Association, had championed the elimination of homosexuality as a disease from the Diagnostic and Statistical Manual of Diseases (DSM). For his now mostly forgotten contributions to humanity, I decided to make Spiegel a main, recurring character in the series.

Though the principal characters in this narrative story are fictitious, I have superimposed their fictionalized history onto the actual events of historical people and real US Air Force units and missions.

The details of the fictional characters' histories are dramatized composites made from the heroic actions of real people, with the details and locations changed to avoid associating any actual person with a fictional character. And though the fictional heroic events may seem unbelievable and overly dramatized, the actual events were even more dramatic in many cases.

The first three books contain abbreviated histories, tracing the technical developments leading to the design of the iconic airplanes with contributions of their lead engineers, as well as the military commanders and units featured in the books.

Though I was encouraged by some reviewers of the first two books to include more technical detail, readers who are primarily interested in following the developing relationship between the two principal characters may find that level of detail too distracting. For those that do, I've tried to limit the deep-dive technical and historical information to the Introduction and the first two chapters of the books so that those not interested in the details can easily skip over them.

Finally, to get a feel for the era's mood, the books reference songs popular at the time of the events. To help readers find and listen to the version of the songs I reference, I've created a music

Thomas Willard © 2021

soundtrack for the series on YouTube of the songs in the order that

they are referenced at

https://youtu.be/MNnUwpMtKQg

and I highly recommend listening to the songs as they are called

out in the text.

Thomas E. Willard   Charlestown, Massachusetts

September 24, 2023

Contents

Introduction 1

Chapter 1 — Nuthampstead Airfield: March, 1944 7

Nuthampstead Airfield 7

The 55th Fighter Group: A Brief History 9

Ramrod to Berlin: Mission Briefing: March 3, 1944 14

Berlin Rendezvous 16

Radio Malfunction 17

Chapter 2 — Rescue 23

No Plan 23

That Was Easy 33

Can't Swim 38

Distraction 43

Landing Lights 45

Passing Out 56

Thomas Willard © 2021

Chapter 3— 49th Station Hospital 59

Ambulance: Bleeding Out 59

Apology 65

Coma 67

Letter from Home 80

Field Promotion 88

Artful Dodger 98

Chapter 4 — Stanbridge Earls Manor, Flak House, Mid-April,

1944 102

Combat Fatigue 102

Flak House 106

Psych Evaluation 108

Nice Dive 128

Swimming Lesson 136

Dancing Lesson 150

The Arrangement 168

Thomas Willard © 2021

Wingmen.. 182

Chapter 5 — Wormingford Airfield: Return to Duty: End of April

1944... 194

Welcome Back... 194

Thomas Willard © 2021

INTRODUCTION

Watching the new P-36 Curtis Hawk fighter being put through its paces at Wright Field on that raw fall morning in 1936, First Lieutenants Benjamin S. Kelsey and Gordon P. Saville were worried: this was the Army's newest and best fighter, the first all-metal mono-wing design, and it was clear from intelligence reports that its competitors would grossly outclass it: the British Supermarine Spitfire, but more importantly, the German Messerschmitt ME109.

Their list of the P-36's shortcomings was long: poor rate of climb, poor roll rate, inadequate armament, poor pilot visibility, a short operating range, non-sealing fuel tanks, insufficient armor plating, a low maximum ceiling, and difficult-to-aim wing-mounted machine guns. But most critically, the plane was slow, almost 100 mph slower than the two foreign aircraft. In a dogfight with an ME109, the two men knew that a P-36 pilot would be at a significant disadvantage. In short, the new frontline fighter hadn't been deployed yet but was already obsolete.

When they reported their findings to the Army Chief of Staff, General George S. Marshall, he ordered them to develop a specification for a new plane: one that would overcome the shortcomings of the P-36 and exceed the performance of any existing or foreseeable foreign design. He wanted a plane that would push the state-of-the-art and would not quickly become obsolete, one that incorporated the latest advances in US aeronautical and engine technology. He wanted the best intercept fighter in the world, and he wanted it within a year.

The two men reviewed intelligence reports of German, Italian, and Japanese fighter designs. They then met with the leading US aircraft and engine manufacturers, along with university scientists, to assess any near-horizon advances to include in a next-generation fighter.

The specification they produced, used to solicit quotes, defined one of the legendary fighters of WWII: The P-38. Its list of accomplishments is astounding.

The prototype, a radical design conceived by Lockheed lead engineer Hal Hibbard and his assistant Clarence "Kelly" Johnson, a 23-year-old who would soon become a legend in his own right, was designed and fabricated in less than nine months. It first flew in January 1939 and then promptly broke the transcontinental speed record, which it held until the end of the war with the introduction of jet aircraft.

It was the first US plane to engage in combat with a German aircraft and was the victor in that dog fight.

Its maximum range, with drop tanks, was 2600 miles, which made it the only US fighter available for bomber escort duty in Europe for the first two critical years of the war, probably saving the daylight bombing program. That range also allowed it

Thomas Willard © 2021

to intercept and destroy the plane carrying Japan's Admiral Yamamoto, the architect of the raid on Pearl Harbor.

Its maximum service ceiling was 40,000 feet, and the time to climb from sea level to 20,000 ft was less than 6 minutes.

Its cluster of a single 20 mm cannon and four .50-caliber machine guns housed in its nose was easy to aim and extremely destructive: the leading US ace of WWII, Richard Bong, flew a P-38 and was credited with 40 kills.

Its twin engines offered a margin of safety versus single-engine planes, and many pilots credited that feature alone for their surviving the war.

And its tricycle landing gear, offering excellent visibility when taxiing, helped prevent taxiing accidents that killed a surprising number of aircrews on both sides of the war.

The plane, though, was complex and challenging for an inexperienced pilot to fly. And its performance was hampered at altitude by an unfortunate mismatch of its pair of counter-rotating Allison 12-cylinder inline engines with GE turbochargers - a

Thomas Willard © 2021

problem later corrected in the P-51 Mustang, which used a Rolls Royce engine with a supercharger. But the plane's design was so forward-looking that it was the only US fighter in full-production throughout the war, with over 10,000 produced.

The plane's last and most crucial characteristic was that it was fast, with a top speed of 465 mph. It was so fast in a dive that the airflow over the wings and control surfaces could go sonic, resulting in loss of control with what became known as "the compressibility problem," which was never fully understood until after the war. At sea level, nothing could touch it, and many pilots survived just by outrunning their pursuers.

For all these reasons, the US pilots who flew the P-38 in WWII came to love her, and they adopted the name her British pilots affectionately gave her for her unmatched speed: The Lightning.

More than 10,000 P-38s were produced during WWII; fewer than five airworthy planes remain today. Like the men that flew her in battle, soon, all will be gone.

Thomas Willard © 2021

WILLARD - LIGHTNING WINGMAN -6

Thomas Willard © 2021

CHAPTER 1 — NUTHAMPSTEAD AIRFIELD: MARCH, 1944

NUTHAMPSTEAD AIRFIELD

Nuthampstead is a small village approximately 15 miles south-southwest of Cambridge, bordering the village of Anstey to the southwest and the hamlet of Morris Green to the east, in Hertfordshire County, UK.

Nuthampstead Airfield, officially known as Station 131, was built just outside the village during 1942-43 by the 814th and 630th Engineering Squadrons of the USAAF. It was built under the terms of the Lend-Lease agreement to standard British RAF

Class A specifications, with three 150-foot-wide concrete runways, 50 loop hardstandings, and two dispersed T2 hangars.

The main runway was 6107 feet long and ran from the southwest to the northeast on a magnetic heading of 045 degrees, in the opposite direction to the prevailing wind. The centerline of the runway was laid out in line with the 60-foot-high spire of the nearby medieval church, St. George's, a half-mile to the southeast in Anstey.

The two converging auxiliary runways were each 4200 feet long and ran 60 degrees to the main runway and to each other. Together, the three runways formed the letter "A," with the main runway crossing the middle of the two diagonal auxiliary runways, which crossed each other at one end, near the top of the "A." A perimeter road encircled the runways, with the outside of the road lined with support areas such as the bomb and fuel depots, and Nissen-hut buildings housing the command headquarters, barracks for over 2500 personnel, the medical dispensary, the mess halls, the enlisted and officers' clubs, and the briefing rooms. There was even a small movie theatre and bowling alley.

The airfield was intended to be used as a bomber base for the 398th Bomb Group, equipped with B-17s, and was the nearest Eighth Air Force heavy bomber base to London, 34 miles to the south-southeast. But it was first occupied from September 1943 to April 1944 by the 55th Fighter Group, which was equipped with P-38s and was the first group to use these aircraft for long-range bomber escort missions. The 398th Bomb Group later took over the station in April 1944 and remained until June 1945.

Besides the military buildings, there was one civilian building within the boundaries of the airfield, the Woodman Inn, built in the 17th century, which served as a meeting place for the American airmen and their local host residents.

#

THE 55TH FIGHTER GROUP: A BRIEF HISTORY

Thomas Willard © 2021

Constituted as the 55th Pursuit Group (Interceptor) on 20 Nov 1940, they were activated on 15 January 1941 and initially trained on P-43s. Redesignated the 55th Fighter Group in May 1942, the Group, consisting of the 38th Fighter Squadron, the 338th Fighter Squadron, and the 343rd Fighter Squadron, converted to P-38s and prepared for combat deployment. They moved to England in August-September 1943 and were assigned to the Eighth Air Force.

On 15 Oct 1943, the 55th Fighter Group became the first P-38 Lightning Group to become fully operational in England. The Group flew long-range bomber escort missions over occupied Europe, racking up 'kills' by destroying enemy aircraft in aerial combat and by strafing them on the ground.

They provided cover for B-17s and B-24s that bombed aircraft plants during Big Week in Feb 1944 and were the first allied fighter Group to fly a mission over Berlin on 3 March 1944.

On 16 April 1944, the Group moved to Wormingford Airfield, USAAF Station 159, about 34 miles southeast of

Cambridge. There, they continued their bomber escort role but also patrolled the skies over the Channel and bombed bridges in the Tours area during the Normandy Invasion in June 1944.

The Group converted to P-51s in July 1944 and were still primarily engaged in escorting bombers that attacked such targets as the gun emplacements during the St. Lo breakthrough in July 1944; industries and marshaling yards in Germany; airfields and V-weapon sites in France; and transportation facilities during the Battle of the Bulge, December 1944-January 1945.

They also patrolled the Arnhem sector to support the airborne invasion of Holland in September 1944 and strafed trucks, locomotives, and oil depots near Wesel when the Allies crossed the Rhine in March 1945.

For their outstanding achievements, the Group received two Distinguished Unit Citations. The first, for eight missions to Germany between 3 and 13 September 1944, when the Group not only destroyed enemy fighters in the air to protect the bombers it was escorting but also descended to low levels, despite the intense anti-aircraft fire, to strafe airdromes and to destroy enemy aircraft on the ground, with a combined total of 106 aircraft destroyed. And a second DUC for operations on 19 Feb 1945, when the Group flew a sweep over Germany to hit railway tracks, locomotives, oil cars, goods wagons, troop cars, buildings, and military vehicles.

The Group flew their last combat mission from England on 21 April 1945, then moved to Germany in July 1945 as part of the occupation forces. There, they were assigned to the United States Air Forces in Europe, training on P-51s and P-80s, until finally being inactivated in Germany on 20 August 1946.

The Group flew over 600 combat missions and was credited with over 303 air combat destroyed-aircraft victories, with 23 probable and 83 damaged. They were also credited with destroying 266 aircraft on the ground, with another 149 damaged. And they destroyed more locomotives by strafing than any other USAAF fighter group in Europe.

But for their most important role, bomber escort, no estimate of bombers saved has been made. The Eighth Air Force bomber loss rate of the mission flown on the day before the 55th became operational was 20%. The loss rate quickly dropped to 5%, and by the end of the war, it was less than 1%.

But probably the best measure of the effectiveness of the escort fighters was the appreciation of the Eighth Air Force bomber crews themselves, who, to a man, credited the courage of the pilots of the 55th and the other escort fighter groups, like the 40th, for their surviving the war.

All these accomplishments came at a great cost, however. Over 198 pilots of the 55th were killed in combat. From a Group with a compliment at full strength of 126 pilots, that was a significant casualty rate. These pilots were the pride of their families and nation; most were just in their late teens and early twenties.

#

Thomas Willard © 2021

RAMROD TO BERLIN: MISSION BRIEFING: MARCH 3, 1944

Colonel Jack Jenkins reviewed the details of the day's mission, another "Ramrod" or deep penetration of Germany escorting B-17 bombers, but for the first time, the target today would be Berlin. On the return, they were to strafe enemy airfields and other targets of opportunity, especially any troop trains heading to reinforce the Atlantic Wall.

Taxiing would be at 0930, rendezvous with the bombers on approach to the target at 1130, escort on return until rendezvous with the P-47 Thunderbolts at 1300 near the Netherlands-German border, then strafing until crossing the Channel near The Hague at 1445, then returning to base at 1600.

The weather at takeoff would be heavily overcast, with a 100-foot ceiling, making the climb to formation treacherous. And on return, a severe storm front was expected to arrive just after landing. As always, an RAF Marine Branch rescue boat would be patrolling the designated sector off Harwich from 1430 until 1630 to rescue any pilots that needed to ditch.

Flight assignments were listed on the mission board. Colonel Jenkins, radio call sign Windsor, would lead the mission at the head of 338th Squadron, call sign Acorn, Orange Flight.

Twenty-year-old sergeant pilot Matt Yetman of 38th Squadron, call sign Hellcat, the youngest pilot in the Group, scanned the board to find his mission assignment.

The flights flew in a four-finger formation, which got its name from the view looking down on the splayed-fingers of a right hand, with the Flight Leader in the long-finger position, followed by his wingman, the Flight Wingman, behind and to his left. Together, they formed the First Element of the flight. The Second Element was formed by the Element Leader, behind and to the right of the Flight Leader, and the Element Wingman, in the smallest-finger position, behind and to the right of the Element Leader. The Element Wingman position was the most vulnerable and was referred to as the tail-end Charlie position – they could be picked off without anyone noticing - so it was always assigned to the most junior, least experienced, and more expendable pilots.

Matt found his assignment, and as expected, he was flying as an Element Wingman, this time for Hellcat Red Flight, behind First Lieutenant Jeff Sullivan, also 20 years old but two months older than Matt.

#

BERLIN RENDEZVOUS

As expected, the weather at takeoff was heavily overcast, and there were several near misses as the Group climbed and formed over the Channel. Not until the Belgium-German border, when the Group had reached 30,000 feet, did the weather clear. By then, half the Group had turned back due to engine troubles: the early-model P-38s had not been adequately tested at high elevation, and their engines often failed due to severe knocking, fuel line freezing, or supercharger problems.

Colonel Jenkins tightened up what remained of the Group and ordered them to jettison their drop-tanks as they approached Berlin. But when they reached the rendezvous area, there were no bombers. When he radioed back to England, he found that the mission had been scrubbed due to bad weather, but through some screwup, Bomber Command had failed to notify Fighter Command.

Still, Colonel Jenkins told the Group they could take satisfaction in being the first Allied fighter group to fly over Berlin, though, because of the absence of the bombers, no enemy fighters chose to engage them. They circled the city twice, and then he ordered the Group to head for home. It was a long way back, and to conserve fuel, he also ordered they should avoid engaging the enemy.

#

RADIO MALFUNCTION

The return flight was uneventful until they neared The Hague when small formations of enemy fighters began to appear. None seemed eager to engage the much larger group of P-38s but were shadowing the Group, ready to jump any stragglers.

When they were in sight of the Channel, Colonel Jenkins noticed what appeared to be a troop train heading southwest. He was frustrated they'd flown the whole mission without firing a shot and was hungry to inflict some damage on the enemy. But the fuel situation was getting critical, and he didn't want anyone to have to ditch in the Channel.

"Windsor to Group. I'd like to get that troop train below at 3 o'clock, but I don't want to risk anyone having to ditch in the Channel. Does anyone have enough reserve to take out the train and still safely make it home? Over."

Jeff Sullivan looked at his fuel gages, then replied, "Windsor, this is Hellcat Red 3. I should have enough. Over."

Matt Yetman looked at his fuel gages and thought he had fuel enough as well, and he was Jeff's wingman. So, for the first time ever, he radioed the Group Leader. "Windsor, this is Hellcat Red 4. I should have enough fuel as well to be able to cover Hellcat Red 3."

"Windsor to Hellcat Red 3 and Red 4. Roger. There are Bandits about, so rejoin the Group as soon as possible. Out."

"Red 3 to Red 4. Break to the right when I do and stay on my tail."

"Roger, Red 3."

With that, Jeff broke hard right, then circled behind the Group before starting his dive on the train, targeting the locomotive. Matt was right behind him, searching all around for bandits.

Jeff pulled out at 100 feet and opened fire on the locomotive. Instantly, the boiler of the locomotive's steam engine exploded, sending large chunks of metal skyward just as Jeff passed over. Pieces hit the engines, causing both to fail.

Thomas Willard © 2021

With no power or elevation, Jeff had very little time to react. He steered towards the only clear ground he could see and crashed just after reaching it.

Matt watched in horror as Jeff's plane went down. It all happened so quickly. His plane was to the right of Jeff's, so he had just missed the debris from the explosion.

He circled back but couldn't see if Jeff had survived the crash. But then he saw Jeff crawl out of the wrecked plane and stand, so he knew he was alive.

Matt's relief didn't last long. The train was less than a 1/2 mile from where Jeff had crashed, and from the way that the Germans were charging, they didn't look like they were in the mood to take any prisoners.

"Windsor to Hellcat Red 4. I saw the crash. Make a pass to strafe the troops if you think you can safely buy Red 3 some time and then rejoin the Group. Over."

But something came over Matt. He had no plan yet, but in that instant, he decided it was unacceptable for Jeff to die, not be murdered like that. He was Jeff's wingman, and it was his job to save him if he could.

"Hellcat Red 4 to Windsor. I think I can get him. Going back for another pass to strafe and figure landing approach."

"Negative, Hellcat Red 4. Return to Group now. That's an order."

But it was already too late. Matt had by then strafed the troops enough to get them to seek cover, buying some time. And he'd formed a plan on how to land. "Hellcat Red 4 to Windsor. Sorry, sir. Radio malfunction." Then he added, "Please don't leave anyone to cover us."

Colonel Jenkins was frantic now. "Hellcat Red 4, do not, I repeat, do not attempt to land." But he could see Matt was lining up to do just that. Resigned to his certain loss, all he could do was add, "Good luck, Hellcat Red 4."

Matt responded, "Thank you, sir," totally blowing his story of a radio malfunction. That prompted most of the Group's other pilots to jump on the radio, offering to cover for Matt. But the

Thomas Willard © 2021

Colonel was buying none of it. "Windsor to Group. Negative on flying cover for him. You're all out of fuel, and I'll be damned if I'm going to lose another one of you.

"I'll shoot you down myself if anyone tries to leave formation. And don't even think about trying that radio malfunction crap again." And then the Colonel, wishing he wasn't in charge and free to fly cover himself, whispered, "Good luck, Matt."

CHAPTER 2 — RESCUE

NO PLAN

Jeff's plane had crashed in a small rectangular field approximately 800 feet long by 500 feet wide. The area was surrounded by trees on three sides and by the southern bank of the Meuse River on the fourth, the longest side.

The trees were tall enough to make approaching from those directions impossible, so Matt would have to approach from the side facing the river. To gain the longest landing strip, he'd have to land in a direction diagonal to the area. Luckily, that direction gently sloped upward.

Jeff's plane was in the northwest corner of the area, so Matt would have to approach from the southeast. But there was a rail bridge - the one the train had just crossed – a half-mile away, blocking the approach from that direction. Matt would have to either go under the bridge or over it and then drop quickly to reach his intended touchdown point on the right heading; the standard 3-degree landing glide slope would be out. He decided to go over the bridge anyway.

The P-38, with its tricycle landing gear, was designed to land only on prepared surfaces. Even landing on a smooth grass field risked burying the nose wheel and flipping the plane over. This was going to be a very hard landing – more like a carrier landing, not that he'd ever made one - on what looked to be alternating patches of soft and rocky ground.

But Matt noticed a rocky outcrop area near his intended touchdown point. If he could touch his main gear wheels down on that, the rock would prevent the wheels from sinking in from the heavy impact load. And if he could keep the nose wheel high until

Thomas Willard © 2021

the speed was reduced to near taxiing, that should prevent the nose wheel from burying itself.

Matt had just passed over Jeff, heading east, but turned sharply south and then west, heading back to the bridge. He lowered the landing gear and selected full combat flaps. As he neared the bridge, the German soldiers started firing their rifles and small arms at him, but at that moment, that was the least of his worries.

He cleared the bridge by no more than two feet, then applied heavy rudder and aileron controls to dramatically crab the plane, using the fuselage as a drag brake and lift spoiler in a forward-slip maneuver. The result was the plane kept on the correct northwest heading but dropped like a stone. At the last possible moment, Matt removed the forward slip, and the fuselage aligned with the flight path just as the main gear wheels touched down on top of the rocky outcrop.

The force of the 10 G impact nearly knocked Matt unconscious while also destroying all the filaments in the radio vacuum tubes and the instrument backlight lamps. But Matt

managed to keep the yoke pulled back and the nose wheel high as

the plane skidded off the outcrop and onto the unprepared surface.

The main gear tires did sink in slightly, but not enough to rotate the

nose wheel over. The combination of the compliant surface and

the upward slope slowed the plane down, though, enough that Matt

thought he might need to add power to reach Jeff. About half way

to Jeff's plane, the nose wheel came down, but at a slow enough

speed to prevent the plane from somersaulting. Though it seemed

like it had been hours to Matt, the total elapsed time from when

Matt had last radioed the Colonel and his landing was less than two

minutes.

Jeff had watched all this unfold in shock and disbelief. The

first thing he saw after he pulled himself out of his wrecked plane

was Matt circling back, diving down to strafe the Germans, and

then climbing, barely clearing the bridge. Jeff thought that would

be it and that Matt would rejoin the Group.

Thomas Willard © 2021

But instead, he watched Matt circle again and then fly over him before circling back to the bridge once more. Again, instead of turning to catch up with the Group, he watched as Matt turned towards the bridge, but this time, he was lowering his landing gear and flaps and looked like he was about to try to land.

At about this time, Jeff became aware of extreme pain in his wrist. The crash had shaken him up some, and he still wasn't thinking clearly, but he suddenly realized his arm was broken when he tried to wave Matt off.

He watched as Matt barely cleared the bridge, then seemed to plunge toward the ground in the most exaggerated forward-slip he'd ever seen. But just before disaster struck, Matt eliminated the slip an instant before the main wheels touched down. And as impossible as it had seemed, Matt was now rolling up to him and turning the plane around, readying it for takeoff.

The Germans had also seen what had happened and were now racing for the planes, firing from still thousands of feet away out of frustration and just to make their intentions clear.

Thomas Willard © 2021

Until that moment, Matt hadn't thought about what landing safely would mean. The P-38 was a single-seat fighter. How were two pilots going to fit?

He could try sitting on Jeff's lap or the other way around. But Matt knew that neither option was possible. He couldn't be that physically close to anyone, especially Jeff.

With the Germans closing in, Matt knew what he had to do. He'd trade places with Jeff. Before Jeff could react, Matt would jump off the rear of the wing and charge the Germans, firing his revolver in hopes that they would shoot him quickly and far enough away to give Jeff a chance to takeoff.

Matt quickly unbuckled his harness, popped the canopy, and climbed out of the cockpit. Brandishing his revolver, he moved to the rear of the port-side wing and was about to jump off when he noticed Jeff holding his obviously broken arm.

Matt's previous plan was now out the window. Matt looked at Jeff and at the advancing Germans, decided all that mattered was saving Jeff, and threw his revolver to the ground.

Thomas Willard © 2021

The P-38 had a boarding ladder housed in the rear of the gondola, but Matt decided there was not enough time to use it. So, he grabbed the back collar of Jeff's flight suit and hauled him up onto the wing.

He helped Jeff move up the wing-root, reached into the cockpit and pulled his parachute, which also served as a seat cushion, and tossed it to the ground. He climbed into the cockpit and then helped Jeff climb in on top of him, with Jeff sitting on Matt's lap facing rearward and with his arms around Matt's neck, supporting his broken arm as best he could.

Matt buckled himself in, pulled the canopy shut, and pushed the throttles wide open, setting all the engine controls to War Military Emergency power.

The German soldiers were getting close now, and they could see that Matt was trying to takeoff, following his previous tracks so his tires wouldn't sink in. So, they diverted their charge in that direction. Matt noticed the change, but also two bandits patrolling above, waiting for him.

Thomas Willard © 2021

The path that Matt was following would take him to the edge of the river bank. If they weren't airborne by the time they reached the edge, they would drop into the river.

If they did manage to get airborne, the bridge would be just in front of them, too tall to climb over. Matt's only other choices were to fly under the bridge or to turn sharply right, upriver, and in the direction of one of the waiting bandits. He decided if he was lucky enough to get airborne, he'd turn right.

Matt could hear bullets striking the armor plating and could see the rocky outcrop fast approaching. He also noticed the outcrop sloped upward. If he could get the nose wheel up enough before reaching the outcrop, he could use the outcrop as a catapult to launch him into the air. Everything now depended on getting the nose off the ground before reaching the outcrop.

Matt began firing his machine guns to clear the Germans out of his way. That worked, and with his speed now over 90 mph and with less than 100 feet to the outcrop, Matt pulled the yoke back and felt the nose rise.

Thomas Willard © 2021

The jolt when the plane's main wheels hit the outcrop was nearly as great as that of the landing, but suddenly they were airborne. Matt immediately retracted the landing gear and flaps and turned hard right, heading upriver. The lower of the two bandits, an FW190, saw him turn and dove to meet him.

Matt was now going 150 mph, heading straight at the bandit, who was going 250 mph. But by turning head-on, Matt had eliminated the speed advantage of the bandit since they were both closing at the same speed.

The P-38 armament, four .50 caliber machine guns, and an automatic 20 mm cannon were all clustered in the nose, so the pilot only had to aim the plane to shoot; the P-38's weapons were accurate for 1000 yards. The FW190 had weapons mounted in the nose and the wings, but the wing-mounted weapons were only effective closer in, at a set convergence point where the line of fire of the cantered guns crossed.

With a closing speed now of over 420 mph and at a distance of less than 3000 feet, Matt opened fire, using all his weapons.

The right-wing of the bandit was blown completely off, and the plane quickly dove into the ground.

There was still the other bandit, another FW190, to worry about, at a higher elevation and coming from the opposite direction. So, Matt warned Jeff, "Immelmann, hang on," as he pulled the yoke back hard, starting the roll-off-the-top maneuver: Matt climbed, pulled a half loop, ended upside down, then rolled 180 degrees to bring the plane back to level.

The result was that they were now nearly at the same elevation as the bandit, heading straight at him and closing at approximately 500 mph.

Again, when the range was less than 3000 feet, Matt opened fire, this time emptying both his .50 caliber machine guns and the 20 mm cannon into the bandit.

Thomas Willard © 2021

The engine of the FW190 immediately burst into flames, and the plane started a steep dive. The pilot may also have been killed, with his finger jammed on the trigger, for he continued to fire straight down until the plane crashed into the river 1500 feet below.

All the while, the German soldiers on the ground kept firing in the vain hope that one bullet would hit something vital. One finally did, but in all the excitement, it went unnoticed until the P-38 was safely heading out to sea.

#

THAT WAS EASY

Matt had watched as the second bandit crashed into the river, about 1/2 mile downstream of the rail bridge. When he looked around to orient himself, he could see the open ocean about 3 miles to the west and began scanning for the lighthouse on Hook of Holland, which he knew from that morning's briefing was the Group's last waypoint before crossing the Channel. The straight-line heading to

Nuthampstead – without the need for a dog-leg to obscure the target of the bombers - from there was due west, 270 degrees true. That heading would also take them over the area patrolled by the RAF rescue boat.

Matt quickly spotted and made for the lighthouse. He climbed to 2000 feet, then set the engine controls to maximum continuous cruise settings, about 275 mph, and as he reached the lighthouse, he turned onto a heading of 270 degrees. Looking in his rearview mirror, he used side-slip until the lighthouse was centered between the twin tails and then, checking his heading one last time, removed the slip. They were heading for their next waypoint, Harwich, England, across the North Sea, about 126 miles or 22 minutes away.

It had been about five minutes since they had taken off, and Matt realized Jeff hadn't spoken a word. And now he noticed that Jeff was shivering.

The P-38 was an advanced aircraft, but the designers had neglected pilot comfort. Cockpit heating was particularly inadequate, especially for a plane designed with a maximum operating ceiling of 40,000 feet.

Matt at first thought that maybe Jeff was just cold. But then he began to worry that Jeff may be going into shock: Jeff had been in a crash and had a broken arm.

From his first-aid training, Matt knew that part of the treatment to prevent shock was to keep the person warm and calm by speaking reassuringly.

Matt was by far the most introverted pilot in the Group, the polar opposite of Jeff, who was the most gregarious, friendly, and outgoing. Matt had always been in awe of how easy-going and friendly Jeff was, and Matt admired him greatly for it.

Jeff knew Matt, only a sergeant-pilot, was shy around officers and had tried more than once to befriend Matt, to get him to come out of his shell. But Matt would always panic and quickly make some excuse, saying he needed to be somewhere else.

Now, to save Jeff, Matt needed to overcome his introverted nature and speak to Jeff and help keep him warm: Jeff's life might

Thomas Willard © 2021

depend on it. So, he thought he'd break the silence with a little gallows humor, saying, "Whew, well, that was easy," as he pulled Jeff closer and began vigorously rubbing his back.

Jeff, who was starting to fade, heard Matt and chuckled a little. In a shivering voice, he said, "Yeah, right. Easy for you, maybe, but not us mere mortals."

Matt, encouraged by Jeff's response, replied with a smile, "Sometimes it's better to be lucky than good."

Jeff, who was starting to feel warmer, half teasingly but still with some seriousness, said,

"That was amazing shooting. Remind me never to piss you off. How'd you do that, anyway?"

Matt thought for a second, not sure how to answer. He knew how extremely lucky they'd been and felt that it wasn't superior skill on his part that had saved them. In the end, he decided to give Jeff an honest answer.

Thomas Willard © 2021

"I just assumed they'd do what I would do. They were very good, and I was extremely lucky; things could have easily gone the other way."

Matt continued to rub Jeff, but it was now as much to comfort himself as to warm Jeff. The images of Jeff's crash and of the rushing German soldiers trying to kill him were still fresh in his mind.

It was only then - after the danger seemed over and the adrenalin had worn off - that Matt began to feel a pain in his left calf. He also noticed wetness in his boot. He looked down at his pant leg and saw a small hole where the bullet had entered and a larger one where it had left. There was no easy way to apply a tourniquet, plus he'd need to keep the mobility and feeling in his leg to fly properly, so he decided to ignore the wound for now. Besides, he was getting closer to the rescue boat and could always ditch if he started to feel light-headed and was in danger of bleeding out.

Thomas Willard © 2021

Jeff's shivering had stopped, and Matt could sense that Jeff was no longer in immediate danger of going into shock. Jeff, except for the pain in his arm, felt strangely comfortable and safe in Matt's arms. He was still groggy and in no condition to make decisions, so he was content to be a passenger, just along for the ride. Plus, there was no way he was going to second-guess Matt, not after what he'd just witnessed. They both fell silent now, but there was no longer any awkwardness between them.

#

CAN'T SWIM

Matt was monitoring his fuel situation. They had enough left to easily make the rescue area, but they'd be lucky to make it all the way home to Nuthampstead. He could try reducing his engine settings to Economy Cruise speed, but bad weather was due to set in, and the fuel saved could easily be lost to fighting headwinds. And it would be getting dark soon. The P-38s had yet to be equipped with radar or any navigation aids except for a compass, so flying at night in a storm was extremely hazardous. The airfield's control tower had radar and could help guide a plane down, but it wasn't something to consider lightly.

That option would require a working radio, so Matt plugged his headset into the receiver but heard nothing, not even static. After checking all the circuit breakers, he realized the radio was dead and probably the Identify Friend or Foe (IFF) transponder as well. That caused the naughty schoolboy in him to smile when he thought to himself, "Colonel, I swear I really did have a radio malfunction."

Losing the radio was bad enough, but losing the IFF meant that, unless some commander on the ground intervened, his plane would be assumed an enemy aircraft and subject to friendly night fighter attack and anti-aircraft fire.

His other option, ditching, had its own problems. Out of necessity, many P-38 pilots had attempted to ditch, but all had died trying except one, who had successfully ditched three weeks earlier. The reasons for failure included planes disintegrating on contact with rough seas and planes sinking too quickly for the pilot to get out. But the main reason was pilots died by drowning from too long exposure to the cold water of the Channel. It was estimated that a pilot had at most three minutes to be rescued or die from exposure. That was the reason for the high-speed RAF rescue boats, which were capable of speeds up to 30 mph. If a pilot could ditch his plane intact close to the rescue boat and get out within 30 seconds, he stood a fair chance of surviving.

These latest developments – low fuel, loss of radio and IFF, and landing in an approaching storm in darkness - changed Matt's assessment. Neither option was attractive, but the risks of continuing to Nuthampstead now seemed to outweigh the risks of ditching.

They were getting close to Harwich now, and Matt could see the RAF patrol boat about 10 miles ahead. He reduced power and began his descent. Without a radio, he wouldn't be able to raise the boat, but he hoped the captain had been alerted to watch for him. The P-38 was an easy plane to identify, and Matt would wing-wave when he got closer to attract the boat crew's attention.

Matt was an excellent swimmer. In fact, he was on his high school swimming and diving team and might have been a candidate for the 1940 Olympics if the world hadn't fallen apart.

He wasn't worried about drowning himself but was worried about Jeff with his broken arm. His plan was to approach the boat at stall speed and ten feet above the water and jettison the canopy just prior to contacting the water. He hoped the slip-stream would carry the canopy cleanly away. He'd immediately try to push Jeff out of the cockpit, then unbuckle his safety harness and join him on the plane's wing. They'd stay there until the plane started to sink, then swim clear. Once in the water, Matt would hold on to Jeff, no matter what, but hoped Jeff could at least keep himself afloat.

Things were happening fast now. Matt wing-waved the boat, then turned to head into the wind. Rather than explain the plan to Jeff, he thought he'd just tell him to follow his directions but not to let go of him. The boat was about one mile ahead, heading for them, and Matt was about to idle the engines when he felt Jeff shaking, much more severely than the shivering before.

"Jeff, what's wrong? Are you ok?"

Jeff tried to answer, but he was shaking so badly that he was hard to understand. Finally, Matt got what Jeff had been trying to say,

"I'm sorry, but I can't swim. I'm terrified of the water."

Matt said, without missing a beat, "Wow, that was close. I should have let you know I can't swim either. I was counting on you to keep me afloat," as he moved the engine controls to Takeoff Power settings and pulled back on the yoke. He began a steep climb to 1000 feet, then leveled off.

They were now approaching land, Harwich, whose lighthouse was the last waypoint until Nuthampstead, actually the spire of St. George's in Anstey, 52.5 miles, exactly 18 minutes at 175 mph, assuming no head wind, on a heading of 280 degrees. Matt found the lighthouse, carefully centered it between the tails while maintaining a 280-degree heading, reduced the engine

controls to Economy Cruise at 175 mph, and then leaned the

mixture a little further. He'd been running on his reserve tanks

since a little past Hook of Holland and knew they were going to

need every remaining drop of fuel to get home.

#

DISTRACTION

Jeff was still shaking violently; whether from being cold, fearful,

or going into shock, Matt didn't know. So, Matt pulled him close

again and started vigorously rubbing his back again. He

desperately tried to think of something humorous to say, but

nothing came to him. But he remembered watching Jeff swing

dancing to Tony Pastor's 1941 hit, "Just for Kicks," at the

Woodman Inn in February when the Red Cross sponsored a meet-

and-greet with the local girls, how happy he looked and thought

maybe that would distract him.

"I saw you swing dancing at the Woodman. You're amazing. How did you learn to do that?"

It took Jeff a moment to process what he'd been asked, but he finally replied,

"I have four older brothers, and they and their girlfriends taught me."

"Wow, four older brothers. You're lucky. I'm an only child. I wish I'd had a brother."

Jeff was shaking less now and felt warmer to Matt.

"Well, you're welcome to any of mine. We all shared the same bedroom. Sometimes, it felt like I grew up in a locker room."

Jeff was feeling better now and understood what Matt was trying to do.

"Actually, I love my brothers very much. I was a surprise baby, so they're a few years older than me. But they never treated me like an infant. I always felt like we were a gang and had each other's back." Jeff then began describing his brothers and some of

the scrapes they had gotten into.

Matt was busy flying the plane and keeping track of time

with the clock on the instrument panel, then using dead-reckoning

to estimate their position. He couldn't afford to be distracted too

much but enjoyed the sound of Jeff's voice, so he tried to keep him

talking by adding an occasional grunt and "uh-huh" while every

now and then looking at the reserve fuel gages, then leaning the

engines' fuel-air mixture just a little bit more.

#

LANDING LIGHTS

When the captain of the rescue boat - part of the fleet of the RAF

Search and Rescue Force, whose motto was "The sea shall not

have them" - first spotted the low-flying P-38 approaching,

obviously intending to ditch, he had adjusted his heading to align

with the wind as the first step in preparing for a rescue. He knew the pilots had been trained to ditch in that direction and as close to the boat as possible.

Once a rescue boat captain could predict the touchdown point, he'd begin to race to that point, with the rest of the crew of eight at the ready to quickly haul the pilot onboard. The captain was about to order full speed ahead when the pilot, just an instant before contacting the water, suddenly aborted the ditching, revving his engines to full and quickly climbing to avoid any obstacles on the nearby shore.

The captain radioed the aborted ditching to Coastal Command, along with the aircraft's identifying markings: CG-J on the booms and a triangle on the tails. The plane had passed so close the markings were easy to read; he'd even been able to see the pilot. He knew from his look-up table that those were the markings of the 55th Group 38th Fighter Squadron. What he also reported, though it seemed impossible, was that it looked like there were two men onboard.

As expected, the weather had worsened when the Group returned to the airfield - with a darkening sky, a 50-foot ceiling, and a strengthening cross wind - so it had taken longer than usual for the Group to land.

Colonel Jenkins, who had waited to be one of the last to land, climbed from his cockpit immediately after his engines had stopped and his wheels were chocked. He raced for the control tower, desperate to let them know he had a possible straggler, maybe 20 minutes behind, with a malfunctioning radio: he didn't want any anti-aircraft guns firing on him. But the report had already come in from Coastal Command that one of his P-38s had aborted ditching off Harwich, that it was now being tracked by the control tower's radar and was about 15 minutes out.

Matt could see he was flying into increasingly bad weather, with darkening clouds and occasional flashes of lightning ahead, but he had no choice; he was now committed to making Nuthampstead; there were no closer airfields.

Thomas Willard © 2021

The gages of both reserve tanks showed only a little more than 10 gallons, maybe 11 gallons, remaining in each. He knew the P-38 on Economy Cruise settings burned a total of 46 gallons of fuel per hour per engine and that he was at least 15 minutes from the base. That already left them shy of one to three gallons of fuel, and that didn't include any fuel for fighting the head wind, which he estimated was now over 20 mph and could add two and a half minutes to this leg of the flight.

The ground was obscured, and he was flying in the clouds on instruments; though none of the backlighting was working, the phosphorescent paint on the needles and numbers made reading them easy.

He knew if they could only make their next waypoint, St. George's spire, they'd have at least a chance of landing safely: he'd memorized the final approach from this direction and felt he could almost land blind-folded. And if he ran out of fuel once he turned on final, there were no obstructions, and he could glide to the runway. He just needed to find the spire in the gloom.

Thomas Willard © 2021

Colonel Jenkins was watching the radar screen along with the controller. Though Colonel Jenkins was the Commanding Officer of the Group as well as the CO of the base, the airfield facility itself and the controller fell under another command. The airfield's runways were equipped with landing lights, which, to prevent targeting from enemy bombers, were designed to be visible only to pilots who were on the correct final approach heading for landing. The lights could only be turned on from the tower and were only used with special authorization from the commander. This directive had been recently emphasized after the airfield had been bombed a week earlier, though the lights had been off, and only minor damage to the base had been done.

Colonel Jenkins knew from having just landed that Matt was flying blind. Without some visual cue from the ground – a flare or lighted runway - Matt would miss the airfield: the runway was only 150 feet wide, and dead-reckoning wasn't close to accurate enough. And he knew he couldn't order the controller to turn the runway lights on. But he and Matt were running out of time.

"So, how do the landing lights work?" he asked, looking at a panel of switches in front of the controller's station.

The controller, suspicious but conflicted, wishing he could turn the landing lights on himself, said,

"These are the switches, numbered 1, 2, and 3, one for each runway."

Satisfied for the moment, Colonel Jenkins returned to the radar screen. But he now knew what he'd do if Matt overshot the field.

Matt watched the clock on the instrument panel as it passed the 18-minute mark since leaving his last waypoint. Under ideal conditions, he should just be arriving at the church spire. He had reduced his elevation to 250 feet relative to the field (the field's elevation was 460 feet above sea level, but the pilots zeroed their altimeters before takeoff). His fuel gages were all reading zero, and the engines were starting to backfire.

Thomas Willard © 2021

He decided to give it two more minutes before turning on final, whether he found the spire or not. Mentally reviewing his landing checklist, he lowered the landing gear, reduced his speed to 150 mph, and lowered the flaps to their halfway position. Then he noticed Jeff shivering again.

Matt knew their situation was desperate, their chances of survival minimal. And he was now starting to feel the effects of blood loss: he felt cold, his vision was tunneling, and his arms, legs, and hands were becoming numb. But he was determined that Jeff was not going to die terrified.

Matt pulled Jeff to him again, but this time when he rubbed Jeff's back, it was gentle and just meant to comfort him. Then, in the most confident voice that he could muster, he said,

"Any minute now. Just waiting for St. George's to show up."

Jeff, when he became aware that Matt was trying to comfort him, responded dramatically. He suddenly felt warm, his shivering stopped, and resigned to his fate, a serenity he'd rarely

Thomas Willard © 2021

experienced before washed over him. As crazy as it seemed, just then, there was no other place on earth he'd rather be.

"Matt, I know we're going to be fine, but no matter what happens, I want to thank you."

Just then, there was a lightning flash, and whether it was just wishful thinking on his part or not, Matt thought he'd caught a glimpse of the church spire to the left below. Thinking he probably only had the fuel in the lines remaining, Matt said, "There she is. Here we go, no worries," and turned onto Final Approach, to a heading of 045 degrees.

An instant before, Colonel Jenkins, who had been staring at the radar screen, decided Matt was going to overshoot the field and lunged for the landing light switch, but before he could reach it, the controller threw the switch himself, saying,

"Sorry, Sir, that's my job," then added, "Sometimes it's better to get forgiveness than permission."

Matt, still rubbing Jeff's back but now humming a tune to comfort him – a tune his mother used to sing to him, the only

Thomas Willard © 2021

memory he had of her - reduced speed to 135 mph, then fully lowered the flaps. He was flying horizontally but descending at a rate of 450 feet per minute on a perfect 3-degree glide slope, assuming the runway was 3000 feet ahead. He was in dense cloud cover and couldn't see anything ahead when suddenly, two diffuse parallel lines of light shone through the clouds below, just slightly to the right of him. He recognized them as the runway landing lights and adjusted his heading to line up with them.

He reduced his speed to 110 mph as he passed over the imaginary "fence" – the unpaved threshold 100 feet before the start of the runway - then broke through the 40-foot cloud ceiling as he pulled back on the yoke, starting his flare and idled the engines. Remembering the cross-wind, he lowered the left-wing slightly, just before his left main gear wheel touched down, quickly followed by the right and then the nose. They'd landed on the letters at the beginning of the runway and on the centerline.

Jeff had been blankly staring into the heavy clouds out the rear of the plexiglass canopy when suddenly he noticed they had

Thomas Willard © 2021

broken into the clear. Just as he turned his head to look forward, he felt the plane touch down and was astonished to find they had landed on the runway.

Matt was still busy flying the plane, trying to keep her centered on the runway. But he was now battling to stop from passing out. All the feeling was gone from his legs, his vision was blurred, and he was losing his sense of hearing. The plane was traveling at 80 mph, still controlled by the control surfaces. He desperately thought, "Not now. Please, just another 20 seconds, and you can take me."

He steered with the rudder pedals by watching his legs; it was too soon to apply the brakes. Finally, the plane's speed fell below 55 mph, and Matt started pressing the tops of the rudder pedals to apply the brakes and to slow and steer, keeping the plane on the centerline as best he could. As he felt himself starting to drift away, he began braking harder, much harder than he normally would.

Thomas Willard © 2021

He could barely see now, so rather than risk veering off the runway, he stood on the brakes to finally bring the plane to a stop. With his last ounce of strength, he reached over and switched the magneto switches to "Off," causing first Engine #1, then Engine #2 to shudder to a stop.

Jeff was now screaming from excitement. Unbelievably, they had landed safely. Matt had somehow managed to pull off the impossible, again, for at least the third time that day. No one would ever believe him when he told them about it.

Jeff was shaking Matt and yelling his name, trying to get him to celebrate with him. But Matt misunderstood him: he thought they must have crashed, and Jeff was crying out in agony. So, searching blindly for Jeff, no longer able to sense his presence, he kept apologizing, repeating, "I'm sorry, I'm so sorry." Then, just before passing out, he whispered, only to himself, he thought, "I love you."

#

Thomas Willard © 2021

PASSING OUT

Jeff was confused, trying to make sense of Matt's collapse, just as a horde of mechanics and pilots arrived and climbed up onto the wings of the plane. They peered in through the canopy first in disbelief, then opened it, flabbergasted to find Jeff had come back with Matt.

But Jeff now knew something was terribly wrong with Matt. One of the faces he spotted looking in was TSgt Wes Potts, Matt's chief mechanic. He told the cheering crowd to be quiet, then said to Wes,

"Something's wrong with Matt. He passed out right after landing."

Wes shined his flashlight into the cockpit and saw a huge pool of blood on the cockpit floor. Then he saw that the left lower leg of Matt's pant leg was soaked with blood.

"He's bleeding; it looks like a lot. The floor is covered. We need to get him out of there fast."

Thomas Willard © 2021

By now, they'd noticed Jeff's arm was broken, and someone had called for a sling so as not to risk injuring Jeff's arm further. But Jeff had no intention of waiting for it.

"You guys need to get me out of here right now. If you don't, I'll get out myself."

When he started to make good on his threat by attempting to stand, multiple arms reached in and pulled him out.

An ambulance had just arrived with the Group's Flight Surgeon, Captain Garnett, the 338th's Flight Surgeon, Captain Randolph, and two medics. They tried to get Jeff to take the ambulance to get him to the hospital as quickly as possible, but he refused, saying, "That's Matt's ambulance. I'll go with him or wait for the next one."

When Jeff asked why they were taking so long to pull Matt out, they said the normal procedure was to apply a tourniquet first, so he yelled,

"Get him out now. They can put a tourniquet on him in the ambulance," and four men lifted Matt out and passed him down to another four on the ground.

They placed Matt on a stretcher and then asked Jeff to lie down on another one: they'd take them both to the hospital together. They put Matt in the ambulance first and had lifted Jeff up when Jeff spotted Wes Potts watching off to the side, looking totally devastated. Jeff knew how close Wes and Matt were, that Wes was probably Matt's only friend, so he signaled to hold off putting him into the ambulance for a second and shouted to Wes, "Sergeant Potts. Wes. Do you want to come with us?"

Wes could only nod yes, so Jeff shouted, "Come on, then," and signaled to the medics that they could continue loading him into the ambulance. Wes climbed in after them, followed by the two doctors, who closed the doors behind them. One of the doctors shouted to the driver, "We're all in," and they sped off with the siren blaring.

Thomas Willard © 2021

CHAPTER 3— 49TH STATION HOSPITAL

AMBULANCE: BLEEDING OUT

The 49th Station Hospital at Diddington Hall was the closest fully equipped USAAF medical hospital to Nuthampstead and was 35 miles away. The drive, now in the dark, on the unlit narrow country roads, would take about 40 minutes.

Doc Garnett and one medic immediately started working on Matt; Doc Garnett applied a tourniquet while the medic checked Matt's vital signs. Doc Randolph applied a splint to Jeff's arm while the second medic checked Jeff's vital signs.

Doc Garnett, whom Jeff had made aware Wes was a friend of Matt's, asked Wes to stand behind Matt's head, near the front of the ambulance, and speak to him in a calm, reassuring voice to let Matt know that he was going to be all right. He also asked Wes to touch him – to place his hands on Matt's shoulders or stroke his hair: anything that might comfort him.

Doc Randolph quickly finished applying the splint and then asked his medic how Jeff was doing. The medic said Jeff's blood pressure and pulse were high but nothing to worry about and that there were no signs of Jeff going into shock.

Doc Garnett finished applying the tourniquet at about the same time and asked his medic how Matt was doing. The medic reported that Matt looked ashen, his blood pressure was very low, and his pulse was high. His breathing was shallow, and he was taking rapid breaths. Doc Garnett knew these were the signs of severe blood loss and that Matt was experiencing a hypovolemic shock. Doc Garnet would try giving Matt plasma, but that plasma was essentially water in Matt's case. What he needed was whole blood with red blood cells to carry oxygen, or Matt would essentially suffocate to death.

Doc Garnett asked what Matt's blood type was, and the medic read Matt's dog tag and said it was O-positive. Then Doc Garnet asked if any of the medics, the driver, Wes, or Doc Randolph, were O-positive, but none of them were, including Doc Garnett. Then the medic, who had constantly been monitoring Matt's vitals, called out, "We're losing him."

Jeff had waited patiently to be asked what his blood type was until the medic sounded the alarm. That was all he needed to hear.

"My blood type is O-positive."

Doc Garnett tried to ignore Jeff, to pretend he didn't hear what he'd said, so Jeff spoke louder,

"My blood type is O-positive."

Doc Garnett didn't want to aggravate Jeff, so he tried to calm him down by saying,

"You can't give blood now. It would put you into shock."

Thomas Willard © 2021

That was just what Jeff was afraid he'd say. As forcefully as he could, he said

"Take my blood, now. Please. I'm begging you. I owe Matt my life ten times over."

But Doc Garnett wasn't about to budge.

"I'd be guilty of medical malpractice if I took your blood now." Then he added, "I can't risk losing both of you."

Before Jeff could reply, the medic interjected, "He's fading fast."

That was it for Jeff. "Take my blood now. I promise I won't go into shock. You can have three people monitoring me, and you can pull the plug if I start to fade. If you don't and Matt dies when we could have saved him, I swear I'll put a gun to my head the first chance I get, and you'll lose both of us anyway."

Doc Garnett, stunned by what Jeff had just said, looked at Jeff and judged that he meant it. "Ok, Jeff. But we pull the plug if your vitals drop, and you promise that you'll never consider making good on your threat if this fails, and we lose Matt."

Thomas Willard © 2021

Jeff just said, "Yes, anything. But please, start right now."

Doc Garnett grabbed the equipment for the direct transfusion from his medical bag and began prepping Matt's and Jeff's arms, then asked the driver to slow down for a couple of minutes to reduce the jarring motion. He inserted the needles and then watched as blood flowed from Jeff to Matt. He had both medics monitoring Jeff and Matt's vitals, with Doc Randolph giving a running report of the results.

Within just a couple of minutes, the medic monitoring Matt bypassed Doc Randolph and said, "He's looking better. Blood pressure is higher." He followed this five minutes later with, "He's looking much better. Blood pressure near normal, heart rate still high, but falling."

Jeff's medic, though, was seeing a different result. Jeff was starting to show signs of distress, with an increasingly rapid heart rate and falling blood pressure. He was about to report this to Doc Randolph, but Jeff read his mind and, in a low, pleading but still menacing voice, said, "Don't even think about it."

Thomas Willard © 2021

The medic, sympathetic to what Jeff was doing, thought that Jeff had the right to risk his life for his friend this way. They did it every day in combat; what was the difference here? So he just nodded ok, that he understood.

Doc Garnett took the change in Matt's condition as a sign that Matt was stable and that he could stop the transfusion. Jeff thought they should take another pint just to be sure but decided not to press his luck.

They were still ten minutes from the hospital, but things seemed to have settled down. Wes, who had watched all this unfold, now had great admiration for Jeff. He knew he'd saved Matt's life at least three times in the span of less than an hour just by the force of his will.

Wes had been gently stroking Matt's hair when he noticed Jeff start to reach across to touch Matt but then change his mind and pull his hand back like he wasn't sure he had the right. Without drawing any attention, Wes grabbed Jeff's hand, guided it to the top of Matt's head, and gently moved it back and forth to encourage Jeff to stroke Matt's hair. Then Wes leaned down and whispered in Matt's ear, "I've been relieved. You're in Jeff's hands now."

#

APOLOGY

As the ambulance neared the hospital's emergency entrance, Jeff withdrew his arm from Matt's side of the ambulance. He was thankful to the doctors, medics, and driver and thought he owed them an apology. He started, "I want to apologize to everyone for …" but was stopped cold by Doc Garnett.

"Lieutenant Sullivan, Jeff, don't apologize; I was wrong and want to thank you. I know everyone here feels the same way. That was the finest display of friendship and courage I've ever seen. I'll remember this ride for the rest of my life."

Jeff looked at Wes, who just nodded in agreement. The doors to the ambulance were opened, and two of the hospital's medics assisted the Group's medics in carrying Matt's stretcher into the hospital. Doc Garnett spoke briefly to one of the hospital

doctors, and then the medics returned to carry Jeff into the

hospital. As his stretcher was being lifted, Jeff turned to Wes and

said,

"Thanks, Wes. I'll try to keep you posted on how he's

doing. Are you going to be all right?"

Wes managed to get out, "I'll be fine. Thank you for

everything."

Then Doc Garnett stopped the stretcher to speak with Jeff.

"You've done everything you possibly could to save Matt.

He's alive because of you. Now, you have another job: to take

care of yourself. I want you to be a model patient, do everything

the doctors tell you, and get well as fast as possible.

"We made a deal, and you promised to do everything that I

asked. I don't want to have to worry about you here."

Doc Garnett then gently grabbed Jeff by his good arm and

said, "Don't worry about Matt. He's gotten the attention of some

very heavy hitters and will receive the best care possible."

Thomas Willard © 2021

With that, the Group's doctors and medics got back into the rear of the ambulance to join Wes for the ride back to base. Jeff couldn't remember making the "model patient" promise to Doc Garnett, but he had no intention of honoring it even if he had.

#

COMA

In March 1944, the 49th Station Hospital was the second-largest US hospital in England. It was located at Diddington Hall, a requisitioned English manor, and had a 750-bed capacity. It was comprised of the Hall itself, which was mostly used to house the medical staff's doctors and nurses, and dozens of Nissen-huts on the grounds behind the manor, housing the Emergency and Operating Rooms, and the support departments like Laboratory, X-ray, and Physical Therapy, as well as the separate patient wards, like Orthopedic, Neurology, Medical, and Surgical.

Jeff was first taken to an Emergency Room, where a doctor examined his arm to confirm that the skin had not been broken and that there was no bleeding or risk of infection. Then, the doctor gave him an injection of morphine and sent him for X-rays.

After being X-rayed, he was taken to the Orthopedic Wing, where a specialist set his arm and put it in a cast. Once the cast had hardened, the doctor checked to see if there was any nerve damage by having Jeff wiggle his fingers. Satisfied there was no nerve damage, the doctor then sent Jeff to the Orthopedic Ward, where the nurses there helped put him to bed. Even though it was only 1800 hours, Jeff, exhausted by the day's events and feeling the effects of the morphine, immediately fell asleep.

Matt was also taken to an Emergency Room, where a team of doctors had gathered to assess his condition. They examined his gunshot wound and found that it was superficial and could easily be repaired with surgery. But the bullet had nicked an artery, so the wound had been a bleeder. Matt had lost about 50% of his blood. His organs didn't appear to have been damaged, but he was now in a coma.

Thomas Willard © 2021

They took Matt to an Operating Room and cleaned and stitched his wound, then bandaged his leg before sending him to the Neurology Ward, where the nurses put him to bed.

Around 0900 the next day, a doctor making his rounds stopped by to check on Jeff. Jeff, who had been wide awake since daybreak, answered all of the doctor's questions while the nurse took his vital signs but was chomping at the bit to ask questions of his own.

The doctor told Jeff he was doing fine and that he wanted Jeff to start Physical Therapy right away that morning if he felt up to it. As he turned to go on to the next patient, Jeff stopped him and then began pummeling him with questions about Matt. Had the doctor heard any news? Was Matt ok? Could Jeff visit him?

The doctor had heard that Matt was in a coma but didn't want to worry Jeff with that now, so he dodged the question. He said he hadn't heard anything about Matt – he wasn't a patient in his ward after all - but would check on him.

Thomas Willard © 2021

Jeff thanked the doctor but didn't quite believe him. So, he bided his time until the doctor had left and then grabbed a nurse as she went by. He asked her if she'd heard any news of Matt, but she gave him the same answer as the doctor. She wasn't as good at deception, though, and Jeff was now sure they were keeping something from him.

So, Jeff switched tactics. He feigned disinterest in Matt and then asked how to get to Physical Therapy and whether he needed an appointment or could just show up. He was anxious to get started.

The nurse was relieved that Jeff's interest in Matt seemed distracted for the moment. She said he could just go over and that she'd arrange for someone to escort him there.

About an hour later, a male nurse appeared, and a very amiable Jeff, dressed in hospital pajamas, slippers, and a terry cloth robe, with his broken arm in a sling, was taken to the Physical Therapy hut.

Thomas Willard © 2021

Once at Physical Therapy, a therapist showed Jeff around, explaining they wanted to exercise all his muscles to keep them toned, even those in his broken arm: being a fighter pilot was a physically demanding job, and they wanted him to be in top condition when his arm was fully healed.

Jeff asked all kinds of questions: what was the best regiment, and should he be worried about re-injuring his arm?

They started him lifting light weights with his good arm, then tried sit-ups. Eventually, his escort got bored and told Jeff to have a nurse call when he was finished, and he'd come back to get him. Jeff, seemingly distracted doing sit-ups, just said, "Sure, thanks," and waved goodbye.

A few minutes after his escort had left, Jeff started asking the therapist questions. Were patients allowed to visit other patients? Were patients free to wander around unescorted? In what ward would someone with a leg wound be located? He did this while smiling and being as friendly and charming as he knew how to be.

Thomas Willard © 2021

The answers were discouraging. Visiting patients was not allowed; it could interfere with patient care. Patients, especially new patients, were supposed to be escorted just in case they had a medical emergency. And the ward a patient was assigned to was determined by his primary care doctor and his condition at admission.

Jeff knew he needed an ally to navigate this labyrinth and was searching for a recruit. He was a pretty good judge of character and thought he'd spotted someone showing an unprofessional interest in him, one of the female nurses.

He made eye contact with her and then called her over to ask for a drink of water. They chatted for a few minutes, exchanging some background information, and then Jeff started to test the water to see if she'd be willing to help.

He started with an extremely brief recounting of the events of the day before without revealing any mission details. He told her how he had crashed and broken his arm, but then how someone had rescued him. How that someone had risked his life multiple times, had bled out, was somewhere in the hospital, and Jeff was sure now needed him. By the end, his eyes were brimming with tears, and so were the nurse's.

He asked if she'd help him find Matt and to escort him there. He was begging now, desperate, all pretense of playing the model patient gone.

The nurse had made her mind up to help. She started by trying to calm Jeff before others noticed and to restore his façade of happy-patient.

She told him a joke to get him to laugh, which he did, but forced, louder than natural. He understood what she was trying to do and that she'd joined his conspiracy. So, he started to relax and pretended to flirt.

She pretended to flirt back but, in a softer voice, told him she needed to check the hospital records to find where Matt was. She asked him to leave for a while to have lunch but to come back in a few hours. She'd call his ward for an escort now, but she'd come to get him around 1300. They'd have to come back to

Thomas Willard © 2021

Physical Therapy first, but she'd take him to visit Matt when her shift was over at 1500, then escort him back to his ward.

Jeff whispered, "Thank you," then asked in a louder voice for her to call for his escort, saying he was starving.

Jeff resumed his hyper-amiable façade, chatting with his escort on the way back to his ward and with the nurses who greeted him with an offer of lunch. Though he had no appetite and his stomach was churning, he ate all of it, just waiting for 1300.

A little after 1300, the nurse-therapist arrived, telling his ward nurses that she and Jeff had arranged for a second Physical Therapy session that afternoon and that she had volunteered to escort him there and back.

When she greeted him by saying, "You ready, sweety?" he gave a smirk for the benefit of the ward nurses, and she escorted him outside. As soon as they were out of earshot, Jeff turned to ask what she had found out.

The therapist-nurse was conflicted. Obviously, Jeff's doctors had decided not to tell him yet about Matt's status. She was going against their judgment if she told Jeff what she'd found out. She decided to tell him anyway.

She told Jeff that Matt was in the Neurology Ward and was in a coma. His other organs seemed fine, but they couldn't tell if he had brain damage. They would give him a few more days before evacuating him to the States. They hadn't notified his family yet.

Jeff was silently sobbing. His worst fears had been realized. He didn't know what to do and had no one else to ask, so he turned to the nurse and begged, "Please help me."

The nurse, in way over her head, looked into Jeff's pleading eyes and considered what they could do. Then, she offered this,

"I'm just a nurse, no doctor. I don't want to give you false hope and make you suffer needlessly.

"But if you promise this would just be about you comforting and saying goodbye to a friend, that you wouldn't get your hopes up and expect a miracle, I'm willing to help.

Thomas Willard © 2021

"I shouldn't be saying this, not with you in such a vulnerable condition, desperate and willing to clutch at any straw. But I've seen many people come out of comas; the ones with the least damage usually come out within a few days.

"What I think helps - and a lot of nurses think so, too, but not all doctors – is someone they know speaking to them in a matter-of-fact voice like they are carrying on a normal conversation. The closer the person is to them, the more private the conversation, with intimate details, the better. And it helps to touch, holding his hand, stroking his hair.

"I have a good friend in his ward. I can smuggle you in now if you promise to behave - no hysterics - and to keep a low profile."

Jeff just turned to the nurse and hugged her, then kissed her on the lips. There was nothing romantic between them, but someone walking past might have had a different impression.

It was a short walk to the Neurology Ward. When they arrived, before going in, the nurse stopped for a moment to make

Jeff presentable. She wiped away his tears, then ran her fingers through his hair, then gave him some final instructions,

"You need to be positive when you go in. You're going to be shocked when you see him, but don't react, at least not out loud or visibly. They don't want you to affect the other patients. If you break down, they'll throw you out and won't let you back in.

"I'll hand you off to my friend, and she'll take you to Matt's bed. She'll bring you a chair and then leave you with Matt.

"You have to be strong for this to work. Are you ready?"

Jeff, not sure if he was ready or not, just nodded yes.

When they went inside, they were greeted by a nurse, whose nametag read "Cowen," who said,

"You must be Jeff, Matt's friend. Remember, he can hear you, so be careful what you say."

Then the nurse escorting Jeff said she had to leave but that she'd be back at 1600 to escort him back. Nurse Cowen then took Jeff to Matt's bed, which was at the end of the row of beds lining the north wall of the hut.

Thomas Willard © 2021

Matt was lying on his back, with his left leg elevated and his arms by his side. He looked to be sleeping peacefully.

The nurse brought Jeff a chair and placed it on Matt's right side, near his head. Then she said she'd be back to check on them both in a while but to call her if he needed anything.

Jeff scooted his chair closer to Matt and then began to quietly speak to him.

"Hey, buddy, how you doing? You're looking good.

"You're in the lap of luxury here in the hospital. It's nice and warm. They're taking good care of you."

Jeff's attempts at banal conversation were quickly running thin. He knew what he wanted to say, so, taking hold of Matt's hand, he did.

"I miss you. You can't leave me. You have to get better. I'm going to go nuts.

"You have to come back."

The nurse noticed Jeff losing it and rushed over.

Thomas Willard © 2021

"Jeff, you have to get hold of yourself. This isn't doing Matt any good."

But all that Jeff could do was look up at her with tear-flooded eyes. He knew he was screwing things up., but he couldn't think any more of what else to do.

The nurse had an idea. It was breaking all the rules, but she didn't care.

"Mail came for Matt today. Somehow, they always know where to find you guys.

"He got a letter from home. Why don't you read it to him? That could help. You should keep reading it to him repeatedly and keep touching him. Stay near to him; he can sense you. And you have to stay strong."

She pulled Matt's letter from her pocket and handed it to Jeff.

"Are you ready to try again?"

Jeff nodded yes. Then, the nurse left him to tend to another patient.

Thomas Willard © 2021

#

LETTER FROM HOME

Jeff tried to compose himself and then spoke to Matt,

"Hey, guy, you got a letter from home from your dad. I'm going to read it to you now."

Dear Matt,

I got the letter you wrote on Christmas. Buster and I went out to Puritan Lawn yesterday to visit your mom and to read it to her. It's always quiet and peaceful there, sitting on the bench in front of your mom's memorial, looking out over the lake. Quiet, that is, except for Buster, who loves chasing all the squirrels up the trees. But he came right back and sat beside me when I started to read your letter. He misses you as much as I do, and I think he might have been able to smell you on your letter.

From the sounds of it, they treated you guys pretty well on Christmas with a turkey feast and a big tree. The way you described the party at the Woodman Inn on base and the Christmas Eve services at St. George's Church nearby, all covered in snow, was something out of Dickens and made me so happy, knowing you were safe and warm and celebrating with your friends. I was worried you'd spend Christmas all alone.

That close friend you mentioned, Jeff, sounds like a great guy. I think you're stretching things a little when you say he's ten times the pilot you are, though; your high school flight instructor thought very highly of you. But I totally accept he's an amazing dancer, especially compared to you: you're terrible, probably because you never had an older brother or sister to teach you, and when it comes to dancing, you take after me. Your mother, though, loved to dance and was very good, so maybe there's hope for you yet. Still, he's got his work cut out for him if he's trying to teach you to jitterbug. I'm just relieved that you've made at least one close friend over there. You've always been a little quiet and shy around people. My biggest fear is that you're all alone.

Thomas Willard © 2021

Mark Twohig, your high school swimming coach, dropped by to check on how you were doing. He said all your old teammates are in the service and doing well. Your closest friend on the team, Peter Kingman, is in the Marines somewhere in the Pacific. His parents got a letter from him a couple of weeks ago saying he was doing fine and not to worry.

I liked Peter very much. He and the coach were very upset when you suddenly quit the team, saying you were going to join the Civilian Pilot Training program. I didn't tell you then, but Peter called me and told me you were avoiding him at school and asked if he had done something wrong. I told him no, and then about the time when you were four when you'd sat on my lap in the rocker in the living room and together, we had listened to the news of Lindberg's flight on the radio, and that ever since then, you'd wanted to become a pilot.

He didn't challenge what I said, but something told me he didn't quite believe me or your reason; I don't blame him. When you both get back, I think you should get together and sort things

Thomas Willard © 2021

out. Whatever is bothering you, you should trust him and let him know. He cares about you a lot and would make a much better sailing partner than Buster, who will never learn to steer or trim the sails no matter how hard you try to teach him.

That reminds me, this season, I had the boat hauled out at the Marblehead Trading Company boatyard and stored inside. The shed is heated, and every Saturday, Buster and I head over there and work on sanding and varnishing the brightwork. It's coming along nicely and should be ready by the start of the sailing season in May. I won't launch her again, though, until you get back. You love that sailboat as much as your mother did, and Buster and I think that if anything will get you to come back home to us safely, that boat will. She'll be right here waiting for you, all shiny and like new, when you get back. I've included a picture of you and Buster returning to the mooring the day before you left for training. You both looked like you'd had a perfect day. I just hope it gets past the censors.

Love, Dad

Thomas Willard © 2021

Jeff was shaking by the time he finished reading the letter. Matt had always been a loner, and his Dad was worried about him. So, Matt had made up a story about some close friendship he had with Jeff. And then he threw in how wonderful Christmas had been, all to ease his Dad's mind. But Jeff could tell his Dad wasn't buying any of it.

Jeff vowed that if Matt recovered, they were going to make everything Matt had told his Dad true. Jeff tried to remember Christmas Day. It was all a blur, but there was no party at the Woodman. They either flew a mission that day or were dead to the world sleeping, recovering from flying long escort missions in some of the worst winter weather England had seen in 50 years.

And he'd discovered that Matt had lied to him about knowing how to swim.

But rather than call Matt out on any of that, he followed the nurse's advice and began reading the letter again.

Thomas Willard © 2021

By the fifth time reading Matt's letter, Jeff started to lose it again. He was choking back tears now, his voice betraying his emotions. Matt hadn't moved or made a sound, and even though Jeff had promised he wasn't expecting a miracle, he clearly was. Now, he was starting to lose hope, and when he got to the part of his and Matt's friendship, he reached the bottom and couldn't go any further.

He was openly sobbing now. He knew he was blowing it, but he couldn't stop himself. So, he just laid his head down on Matt's chest and surrendered to his grief, waiting to be shown the door.

Matt thought he was dreaming. He could hear Jeff crying out to him but wasn't sure where they both were. He could hear other voices around him, but except for Jeff's, he didn't recognize any of them. Someone - a woman with a vaguely familiar voice - was gently saying, "You have to go back now; he needs you," but go where and who needed him. He opened his eyes and couldn't make out where he was, but felt and then saw Jeff with his head on his chest, sobbing. So, he reached over to place his hand on his head to comfort him.

Jeff slowly became aware that someone had placed their hand on his head but was too distraught to look to see whose it was, figuring it was probably just a nurse about to ask him to leave. But the angle was wrong for that, and then he felt the same magical feeling he'd felt the day before when Matt had comforted him. Jeff realized that, incredibly, the hand was coming from the person in the bed.

Matt still thought he was dreaming, but when Jeff stared at him in shocked disbelief, he started to panic: this was no dream.

Jeff, seeing the fear on Matt's face, started babbling,

"It's ok, Matt. It's me, Jeff. You're safe here in the hospital."

By now, the nurses were all rushing over, followed by a doctor. But Matt only saw Jeff. "You're safe? You didn't burn in the crash?"

Thomas Willard © 2021

"No, Matt, I'm good. Really good now! There was no crash. You made a perfect landing."

By now, Jeff was being pushed aside and had lost hold of Matt's hand. The doctor roughly asked, "Who's this?" pointing at Jeff. So, Nurse Cowen told him he'd have to leave now and escorted him to the entrance.

Before he left, Jeff gave Matt's letter back to her, saying, "Please give this back to him. And thank you so much; you saved his life."

Nurse Cowen kissed Jeff on the forehead and said, "I didn't, but you did," then added,
"Don't worry about him. He's weak as a kitten, but he'll be fine now. I'll try to get word to you on how he's doing."

Jeff walked back to Physical Therapy and found the nurse-therapist who'd helped him. He told her that Matt had regained consciousness and asked her to escort him back to his ward.

When they got there, he stopped at the entrance and thanked her for saving Matt's life. Like Nurse Cowen, she

Thomas Willard © 2021

protested that it wasn't her who did the saving, but this time, Jeff was adamant.

"No, it was you, all you. I can't thank you enough for saving Matt and for all your compassion when I desperately needed help.

"I know it's a lot to ask after everything you've already done, and I don't want to get you in any trouble, but could I hold you for a minute?"

She could see Jeff was shivering and no longer cared what anyone passing by would think, so she gave her answer by wrapping her arms around him, whispering in his ear, "Anytime. But no worries, OK? I know you're in love with somebody else."

#

FIELD PROMOTION

The next day, they moved Matt from the Neurology Ward, filled with patients with the most severe head injuries, to the Medical Ward, with the less critically wounded patients.

Thomas Willard © 2021

Word had reached back to the Group, to Doc Garnett, that Matt had regained consciousness, and the Doc had passed the information to Colonel Jenkins, who then told the 38th Fighter Squadron's Commanding Officer, Captain Hancock, who then shared it with the rest of the men in his squadron. But by then, Colonel Jenkins had made a special trip to Hangar #2 to personally let TSgt Potts know that Matt was out of danger.

Colonel Jenkins waited a few days for some paperwork to be processed, then drove himself to visit Matt in the hospital. He found Matt resting but not sleeping and quickly waved off Matt's attempt at rising to salute.

The beds in the ward were in the open, with no privacy curtains, but the Colonel ignored that and decided to speak plainly. He started,

"How's it going, Matt? You're looking good. I know you're still pretty weak, so there's no need to answer. I'll only stay a minute.

"First, you had just missed the minimum cut-off age for being an officer by two weeks before we came to England. You're only two months younger than Lieutenant Sullivan and the other pilots and should never have been made a sergeant pilot. So, I'm promoting you to First Lieutenant, effective immediately. You're well over the minimum age now and should have already been promoted to Second Lieutenant – just an oversight on our part, no reflection on you – so we're skipping over that rank.

Before Matt could object – he wanted no recognition for rescuing Jeff – the Colonel, anticipating Matt's objection, added, "This has nothing to do with the Berlin mission. It's what should have already happened." Then, he waited to gain his composure before continuing.

"Second, I'm putting you in for the Congressional Medal of Honor. In your application, I wrote your bravery, skill, and heroism is unmatched in my personal experience. I meant every word of it. Besides, if I don't put you in for it, the whole Group will mutiny against me. You don't want that, do you?"

Thomas Willard © 2021

Colonel Jenkins expected Matt to object – Matt was the most unassuming, modest person he knew, a rare personality for a pilot – but was totally unprepared for Matt's reaction.

Matt started wailing, pleading with the Colonel not to put him in for the Medal. He said that he'd only done what any of his other pilots, any wingman, would have done. He begged not to be singled out. Then, sensing he wasn't winning the argument, reminded the Colonel that he'd disobeyed a direct order and should be court-martialed, not promoted, or honored with a medal, especially not that medal.

Colonel Jenkins considered everything Matt was saying but was moved more by Matt's emotional response than by his words. So, he offered a compromise.

"I checked with your chief mechanic after you landed, and your radio was out, so as far as I'm concerned - and I'm the only one that matters here - you did not disobey any direct order.

Thomas Willard © 2021

"Matt, I was looking forward to you getting the Medal and having the privilege of saluting you first. But it seems like I'm not going to get that honor.

"I'll make you a deal. When we meet, you give me an instant to salute you first. Nobody else needs to know; it will just be between you and me.

"I won't turn your paperwork in for the Medal, but I'll keep it in my desk drawer just in case you decide to renege on the bargain. Agreed?"

Matt just nodded yes. Then the Colonel added,

"Your other paperwork is all processed, so you're keeping the promotion. No arguments. Do you want to screw up the whole system?" Then, he thought to himself, "Not to mention, General Doolittle would have my hide."

Colonel Jenkins reached into his pocket and pulled out a pair of First Lieutenant silver bars that he had once worn and handed them to Matt. "Here, you're going to need these when you get out of here." Then he remembered he'd brought something else.

"Oh, I almost forgot; TSgt Potts asked me to give you this," and pulled out a small box. Inside was the Lockheed logo medallion from the center of the P-38's yoke. Wes had drilled a small hole in it near the edge and attached a string of rawhide so it could be worn over the neck. On the back, he'd inscribed,

Matt, this was the only salvageable piece from your plane, and I thought you'd like to have it. Get well soon, Wes. P.S. Trust Jeff in all things; I do.

Colonel Jenkins knew Matt was worried about his line crew, so he told Matt that he wasn't going to reassign them to another pilot. They were in training now and filling in to help other crews. He'd be giving them leave in a few weeks, but they'd all be there waiting for Matt when he got back.

Then, the Colonel lowered his voice and whispered, "Your Dad should be very proud of you. I've written him a letter saying that it's an honor to serve with you and that you are a credit to the

Group. It's already been mailed, so it's too late to do anything about it; you'll just have to live with it." Then he quickly rose to leave before he lost control, but not before turning back and saluting Matt, who quickly returned the salute.

Colonel Jenkins then searched for Jeff and found him in bed, speaking with the patient in the next bed over. He first asked Jeff how he was doing, then told him he had just visited with Matt and about Matt's promotion, and then decided to share Matt's refusal to accept the Medal.

Jeff vigorously argued for Matt to receive the Medal. He recounted everything that had happened during the rescue flight: the unimaginably difficult landing and takeoff, the two bandits destroyed, the aborted ditching when Matt learned Jeff couldn't swim, the dead-reckoning in the dark and the heavy cloud-cover, flying on fumes, and the low-ceiling night landing with a strong crosswind, all while bleeding-out.

Colonel Jenkins, who'd only known that Matt had somehow managed to rescue Jeff, had aborted ditching for some reason and had done all this while wounded, was stunned. He agreed with Jeff that Matt now more than ever deserved the Medal but had just experienced Matt's near-meltdown when he'd told him he was being submitted for the Medal.

In searching for Matt, Colonel Jenkins had stopped at the Neurology Ward first since that was where he'd been told Matt was located. There, the nurse that had attended Matt told him they had just recently moved Matt to the Medical Ward, and she offered to take the Colonel to him. Along the way, the nurse told him about the great lengths that Jeff had gone to help Matt regain consciousness and that, in her opinion, Jeff had saved Matt's life.

Doc Garnett had also told Colonel Jenkins about Jeff's insistence on giving blood during the ambulance ride to the hospital - despite the real risk of his going into shock - and his threat of killing himself if he didn't comply. Doc Garnett told Colonel Jenkins that Matt would certainly have died in the ambulance without Jeff's intervention.

Thomas Willard © 2021

Colonel Jenkins now thought that both men deserved the Medal. From what he could see, they had acted as a team and had shown total disregard for their own lives to save the other. So, the Colonel decided to throw the rulebook out the window.

"Jeff, I know about everything that you did, from when the plane first touched down, to save Matt, including what happened in the ambulance and what happened here. Matt owes you his life many times over, and from what you just told me, you owe your life to Matt just as much.

"You two guys are now joined at the hip to me, two sides of the same coin. I don't feel comfortable deciding what's best for either of you on this. And right now, I care more about what's best for you two than what's best for the Army. So, I'm going to leave this decision to you - you have more of a right to decide than me. But just to let you know, I think you deserve the Medal as much as Matt."

Jeff didn't feel like a hero and didn't want a medal. He'd already gotten what he wanted: Matt was safe. Then he realized that was how Matt probably felt. He explained that to Colonel Jenkins, and they agreed to let the Colonel's agreement with Matt stand. Then, instead of saluting Jeff like he had Matt, the Colonel shook Jeff's hand, thanking him for saving Matt's life, saying, "I know you'll take good care of him," before leaving.

Matt and Jeff never saw Colonel Jenkins again. Five weeks later, he was shot down by flak leading a low-level strafing mission on a well-defended airdrome in France. He survived the crash and spent the remainder of the war as a POW.

****

Lieutenant Colonel Jack S. Jenkins was the first US pilot to engage a German plane in combat in WWII and, flying a P-38, had shot that aircraft down. He also led the first Allied fighter bomber-escort mission to Berlin and returned to Berlin several more times before being shot down in France. He flew 70 combat missions in a little over five months, was awarded the Distinguished Flying Cross in January 1944, and was credited with two fighter aircraft destroyed, one probable, and one damaged. At the time he was

Commanding Officer of the 55th Fighter Group, he was just 29 years old.

#

ARTFUL DODGER

For the next two weeks, both Matt and Jeff, apart from their daily Physical Therapy sessions, were mostly confined to bed. Matt's leg wound was quickly healing, and his strength was coming back, and Jeff's arm, a simple fracture, was on the mend. Both were on a path of full recovery that would have them released from the hospital in six weeks, by the second or third week of April.

The nurse-therapist kept Jeff briefed on Matt's progress, but all the news was good, so Jeff began to relax his hyper-vigilance, even forgetting some days to ask how Matt was doing.

As their condition improved, they were allowed to walk the grounds but still escorted and in small groups. Matt and Jeff would sometimes see each other from a distance and wave, but that was as close to visiting as they got.

Starting about the fourth week, they could dine in the patient's mess hall, but only at their ward's assigned times, and were required to stay in their ward's assigned section. Their two wards were on different dining schedules, so it was rare for them to see each other then.

During their fifth and sixth weeks, they were allowed much more freedom and could roam the grounds unescorted and eat in the mess hall anytime it was open in an unreserved section. This was when things began to unravel for Jeff.

Jeff had sent several messages to Matt by way of the therapist-nurse's network of friends, suggesting a time for them to meet at the mess hall or to just walk the grounds. But Matt always had an excuse and was never available. So, Jeff hatched another plan. He'd figure out Matt's schedule with the help of his nurse-spy network and ambush him.

Matt always got up early and ate breakfast when the mess hall first opened at 0600. On the Wednesday morning of their sixth week, three days before Matt was scheduled to be released and four days before Jeff was, Jeff got up at 0530, dressed, walked to the mess hall, and positioned himself so he couldn't be seen by Matt until he was at the mess hall door. Sure enough, at 0600, he saw Matt approaching and heard the mess hall doors opening. As casually as he could, he walked into Matt's view and said, "Hi, Matt. You're up early."

Matt, still six feet away, was startled to see Jeff. His reaction was a confusing mix of unbelievable joy at seeing him, excruciating shame and embarrassment, and total terror and panic. He had been trying to avoid Jeff – he'd remembered what he'd said to Jeff before passing out - and it looked like Jeff was about to confront him with it.

The first thing that Jeff noticed was that Matt's face was flushed crimson. He also noticed Matt wouldn't look him in the face. It seemed that Matt had reverted to his withdrawn shell, and despite all they'd been through together, the original awkwardness between them had returned.

Thomas Willard © 2021

Jeff's instinct was to grab Matt and hold him until he squeezed the awkwardness out of him. But he didn't. He was too devastated to find that the month they'd been separated had given Matt time to build his defensive walls back up. Jeff could see that Matt was in great discomfort, so rather than cause him any more pain, he said, "It was great seeing you, Matt. Take care," and left.

What Jeff couldn't have known is that had he closed the short distance between them and held Matt in his arms, he'd have found a very different Matt, the one he was desperate for, waiting, eager to return the embrace.

CHAPTER 4 — STANBRIDGE EARLS MANOR, FLAK HOUSE, MID-APRIL, 1944

COMBAT FATIGUE

After its disastrous first battle with the German Army, in what became known as the Tunisian Campaign in North Africa, the US Army realized it had a serious problem. The horror of the battle had been too much for many of its untried troops, and after witnessing unimaginable carnage, many of the soldiers had mentally broken down and were unfit for service; 20% of these were judged so bad they had to be sent back to the States. The Army commanders knew they couldn't sustain this high of a casualty rate due to what they called "combat fatigue" and win the war. They needed a solution quickly and turned to their combat fatigue chief expert, neuropsychiatrist and psychoanalyst Colonel Roy Grinker, US Army Medical Corps, who was luckily already in the field.

Colonel Grinker immediately sent for his associate, psychiatrist Captain John Spiegel. Together, they studied the problem and developed a program of prevention and a treatment regimen that ultimately resulted in returning over 70% of combat fatigue patients to duty. The release of their final report to the Army, "War Neuroses in North Africa: The Tunisian Campaign, January to May 1943", and the quick adoption of their recommendations by the Army was a watershed moment in the treatment of combat fatigue.

Until Grinker and Spiegel's report, the US had accepted the British view that combat fatigue was due to a "lack of moral fiber" and could be prevented by careful screening of recruits. But, after interviewing their combat fatigue patients in Tunisia, Grinker and Spiegel came to a different opinion.

Grinker and Spiegel saw combat fatigue as a natural, human result of exposure to the extreme horrors of war: that the results accumulated with exposure and were aggravated by exhaustion, cold, and hunger, and that every human being had a limit, a breaking point, that would predictably result in breakdown and should not be allowed to be exceeded. They turned the question of breakdown around, from asking, "Why did some men break down?" to "Why didn't everyone break down?" Their answer was that breakdown could be prevented in an average soldier if the human exposure limit to the unremitting and horrendous stresses of war wasn't exceeded and depended on the respect and regard the soldier held for his officers, his trust in his training and equipment, but more importantly, the strength of the emotional bonds between him and his fellow soldiers and the officers closet to him in his unit.

Their treatment for patients was surprisingly simple but proved extremely effective. New patients, far from the front, were first given a warm shower or bath, good food, a comfortable bed, and then a heavy dose of sodium pentothal to induce sleep for two days. They were then allowed a period to relax and rest, with no military duties. When it was decided they were up to it, they were invited to join a group of combat fatigue patients, where they were encouraged to share their traumatic experiences.

This simple prescription - lots of rest, good food, a warm, clean bed, and group therapy – led to a full recovery for over 70 % of patients, often within as little as ten days.

To prevent combat fatigue, Grinker and Spiegel recommended limited exposure to extreme combat conditions, recovery periods after exposure, monitoring and weeding out of "stressed" individuals, and as much relaxation and leave as possible. Open discussion and admission of fear were to be encouraged, even joked about, and eliminating any shaming for showing signs of combat fatigue.

Thomas Willard © 2021

When the Army evaluated the results of the treatment of the Tunisian combat fatigue soldiers, they were convinced of the treatment's effectiveness and ordered that Grinker and Spiegel's recommendations be immediately implemented in all combat Theatres of Operation.

To help train the Medical Corps psychiatrists in the new approach, Grinker was temporarily assigned to the US 5th Army, then fighting in Italy, while Spiegel was assigned to the US Eighth Air Force in England.

#

FLAK HOUSE

To provide a place for USAAF combat aircrews to recover from the effects of combat fatigue, a series of rest homes were established in the English countryside, mostly in the large manor homes of the landed gentry. Eventually, seventeen of these homes, affectionately called by the stressed airmen, most of whom were almost daily exposed to anti-aircraft fire, Flak Houses, were provided by the British to the USAAF. One of the first was Stanbridge Earls Manor, about a half-mile northwest of the town of Romsey, in the county of Hampshire, and about 69 miles southwest of London.

The Manor could accommodate up to 30 officers, mostly pilots, providing individual rooms for privacy to most. As was standard for all the rest homes, there were cooks and housekeepers and two Red Cross women to provide platonic companionship: to dance, play cards, or just chat. The airmen were provided civilian clothing, rank was ignored, and any military conversation was discouraged. The airmen were free to wander the grounds, fish, ride horses, or bicycle to the local town of Romsey.

Airmen were usually sent to the rest homes midway through their tour of duty or whenever signs of combat fatigue appeared. Squadron Flight Surgeons had the most say in determining when a pilot needed rest and would generally prescribe a period of ten days or more. Any pilot that suffered a traumatic incident – had crashed or seen a friend shot down – was usually immediately sent to a Flak House, as was any pilot that had just been released from a hospital.

Before any airmen could return to duty, they needed to be evaluated by a visiting psychiatrist. The psychiatrists rotated between the Flak Houses and were usually assigned to the closest General Hospital. The closest to Stanbridge Earls was the 303rd General Hospital, which also happened to be the training hospital for all US Army Medical Corps psychiatrists in England.

#

PSYCH EVALUATION

Captain John Paul Spiegel was a US Medical Corps psychiatrist and an expert on combat stress. He usually didn't visit the Flak Houses himself but provided training to the psychiatrists who did and to the flight surgeons so they could evaluate airmen for signs of stress.

He'd recently given training to the 55th Group's flight surgeons and was approached by one of them, Captain Garnett, after the training, who asked for a private meeting.

Doctor Garnett said he needed help evaluating the fitness of two pilots that were a concern. They had been through some harrowing experiences together, avoided death multiple times in quick succession, and had both been wounded but weren't showing the normal signs of combat fatigue. But before he revealed what his concerns were, he wanted Captain Spiegel's assurance that he'd consider the conversation private and that no notes or records of any kind would ever be made.

Captain Spiegel realized that it had been extremely difficult for Doctor Garnett to approach him. Doctor Garnett was torn between the safety of his pilots and his duty to the Army. But he was also worried about the mental health and reputation of his pilots. Captain Spiegel thought Doctor Garnett doubted his own objectivity and medical judgment because he cared for these pilots so much.

"These pilots mean a lot to you, don't they? Otherwise, you wouldn't have approached me like this. And I think you're worried that someone not as close to these pilots as you are, and a stickler for adhering to Army regulations and societal norms, might ruin these pilots' lives. Am I close?"

Doctor Garnett was amazed at how perceptive Captain Spiegel had been. So, he took a chance, "Yes, you've hit the nail right on the head."

So, Captain Spiegel tried to assuage Doctor Garnett's fears.

"I'm an independent thinker, basically a heretic. If I wasn't, we'd still be stuck with the British view that combat fatigue was due to poor character. We've proven that's baloney.

"I think psychiatry is still in its infancy, and many of its practices are just wrong, barbaric even, like doing lobotomies or giving electric shock therapies to homosexuals. Right now, its goal is to make patients adhere to societal norms, no matter what damage it inflicts on them. Its goal should be to make the patient as happy as possible, comfortable living in his own skin, within the bounds of not hurting himself or others.

"Societal norms are not absolute: they change, sometimes too slowly, but tend to drift towards a more humane, understanding world. I just hope that in my lifetime, I can somehow contribute to speeding that evolution along.

"I hope that answers your concerns, and I swear I'll take everything you tell me to the grave."

Relieved beyond measure, Doctor Garnett said that Captain Spiegel had more than allayed his concerns and thanked him for his candor. Then he told him about the rescue flight, how Matt multiple times had selflessly risked his life for Jeff, only for Jeff to do the same thing for him. He told Captain Spiegel about Jeff's threat of suicide to extort Matt's transfusion from him and even related the story Colonel Jenkins had told him of the lengths that Jeff had gone through in the hospital to help Matt regain consciousness.

Finally unburdened by the weight of carrying his concerns alone, Doctor Garnett asked if Captain Spiegel would be willing to evaluate both Matt and Jeff and give him his opinion of whether they were fit for duty. He'd scheduled both for a stay at the Stanbridge Earls Flak House after they were released from the hospital the second week in April.

Captain Spiegel agreed to do the evaluations and said he'd use combat fatigue as the reason if he decided one of them or both were not fit for duty. Then, he joked it may not be the real reason, but who was going to argue with the guy who wrote the book?

But Captain Spiegel had a condition of his own. If, while doing his evaluations, he discovered any personal information of a moral nature that may be of interest to the Army, he had no intention of divulging it to the Army or to anyone else, including Doctor Garnett.

Doctor Garnett just smiled and said, "No worries. And good luck on your "speeding evolution along" goal. I'm rooting for you."

Matt arrived at Standridge Earls on a Sunday, a day before

the usual rotation of airmen, so he had to share a room with

another pilot, also from the 55th. He was told, though, that he'd be

given his own room as soon as a single became available. He was

also told he'd be interviewed by a visiting psychiatrist, Doctor

Spiegel, sometime later in the week.

Jeff arrived the next day around 0900 and was assigned a

recently vacated single room. He asked for Matt but was told he'd

already left to visit Romsey and should be back in time for supper.

Around noon, Captain Spiegel arrived and was shown to

the visiting psychiatrist's office. He had taken a night bag with him

and asked if there was a spare room available; if not, he'd sack out

on the couch. They had a spare, and he went there to change into

his civilian clothes: he didn't want to stand out.

Usually, the visiting psychiatrist would evaluate all the

airmen staying in the house, but Captain Spiegel made

arrangements so that he was only going to evaluate Matt and Jeff,

though he didn't want it known that the two had been singled out.

Thomas Willard © 2021

He went to the main lounge area and asked one of the Red Cross women if she knew Matt or Jeff and if either one was there. She pointed to Jeff reading in a high-back chair in a corner and offered to introduce him to Jeff. But he told her no, he'd introduce himself later. She told him Matt was out. He asked her to let him know when Matt returned but not to tell Matt he'd been asking for him. She knew he was the visiting psychiatrist and probably wanted to observe Matt and Jeff before evaluating them, so she agreed.

They served lunch, and then more guests arrived, bused there from the nearby airfields. Around 1700, the main door opened, and Matt appeared. Jeff, who had positioned himself to see anyone arriving, immediately got up and walked toward Matt. Captain Spiegel noticed someone entering and Jeff rising to greet him, so he correctly assumed it was Matt.

What he didn't expect was Matt's reaction. From his body language, Captain Spiegel could tell that Matt was defensive and could see that he was trembling.

Thomas Willard © 2021

Jeff, who was obviously desperate to speak to Matt, offered his hand, which Matt quickly took to shake but just as quickly dropped. Jeff asked if he'd be around for supper, but Matt said he'd already eaten, was tired, and was probably going to bed.

Dejected, Jeff said, "OK, see you tomorrow," and left out the main door. Captain Spiegel thought, "Always get the quiet ones when they're upset; they can't lie as well, then." And then, "I hate my job sometimes."

As Matt started to climb the stairs to his room, Captain Spiegel approached him.

"Hi, Matt, right? I'm Captain John Spiegel, a doctor from the 303rd. They probably told you I'd be here this week to interview you.

"I overheard that you'd already eaten, and I have a full day tomorrow. Do you think we could do the interview now and get it over with?"

The answer Matt wanted to give was no, but he had little strength to argue, so he agreed.

Thomas Willard © 2021

Matt followed Captain Spiegel into his office and sat in the chair in front of the desk. Captain Spiegel closed the door behind him, but instead of going behind the desk to sit as Matt expected, he sat on the edge of the desk in front of Matt, purposely crowding him. Captain Spiegel began,

"So, Matt, how's it going? Are you enjoying your stay here so far?"

Matt nodded and said everything was fine but offered nothing else. So, Captain Spiegel, knowing the interview was going to be difficult for Matt, decided not to delay things and began his assault.

"I have to ask you about your rescue mission. That was amazing, but it seemed a tad reckless on your part. And did you have to do all the work, or was Jeff any help at all?"

That set Matt off big-time. He started by yelling about how great a pilot Jeff was and that unless Captain Spiegel was a fighter pilot, he didn't have a clue, and his opinion didn't count. He said that Jeff had made every decision on the flight, and Matt wouldn't be sitting there without his help. Jeff deserved the Congressional Medal of Honor; Matt was just along for the ride.

Jeff was a great guy, the most friendly, generous person he knew. And probably the best dancer in the whole world, and... and then he abruptly stopped. He just folded his arms, glaring at Captain Spiegel, defiant.

Captain Spiegel had his answer, though it pained him what he'd had to put Matt through to get it. Before he let Matt go, he thought he'd try to calm him down if he could.

"I apologize; I was wrong to ask the question the way that I did. I know Jeff is a great guy, by some things that he did for you while you were unconscious and don't know about yet. He cares about you a lot, and it's obvious by the way you rose to defend him just now that you care a lot about him, too. I'm sorry I upset you."

Matt, trying to calm himself down, had pulled his medallion through the buttons of his dress shirt and was staring at the inscription on it, tracing the engraved words with his finger.

Thomas Willard © 2021

Captain Spiegel noticed the inscription and asked to read it. Reluctantly, Matt obliged, pulling the medallion farther away from his chest and holding it out so Captain Spiegel could read it.

When he'd finished reading the inscription, Captain Spiegel asked, "Who's Wes? He seems like a good friend."

Matt, loathe to share any personal information with Captain Spiegel but proud of his friendship with Wes, replied, "He is; he's a very good friend."

Captain Spiegel, in a gentle and sincere voice, replied, "I think he must be, and pretty wise, too. Why don't you take his advice?" Then he told Matt he could go.

Jeff was up at 0630 and had just finished breakfast when Captain Spiegel, still dressed in civilian clothes, approached him.

Again, the Captain started, "Hi Jeff, I'm Captain John Spiegel. I'm here to evaluate you so we can send you back to your base. Is now a good time?"

Jeff said sure, he'd just finished breakfast, so he was free, and then followed Captain Spiegel into his office. This time, after

Thomas Willard © 2021

Captain Spiegel closed the door, he sat in the chair behind the desk. Captain Spiegel came right to the point,

"Jeff, I've got a problem. I've been asked to evaluate you and Matt to see if you're fit to return to duty.

"I've already interviewed Matt, and it didn't go well. I have the authority to send Matt back to the States, where he'd be safe. I don't think that would make him happy. But here, right now, I'm worried he could be a risk to himself.

"I saw your interaction with Matt yesterday, how he avoided you, pushed you away, and how devastated you were. But you weren't here when I interviewed him immediately afterward, so you don't know how he really feels about you.

"I have a theory of why he's behaving like he is towards you. I'm violating all my medical ethics by sharing it with you or discussing Matt in any way, but I'm putting all that aside.

"However, I also need to consider what's best for you, too. So, I need you to trust me and tell me the truth about what you really want. You don't know me; why should you trust me? So, I'll go first. As I said, they could have my medical license, court-martial me, and throw me out of the Army for what I'm about to tell you, so hopefully, you'll trust me after I share my thoughts with you.

"From what I can see, there are only four options for Matt.

"The first option is I could send him back home, where he'd be safe. I know you want him to be safe, so you might favor that option. I think it would be bad for the Army and Matt if I do that, though, unless Matt remains a threat to himself.

"The second option is you both could return to your base and pretend like the rescue flight never happened. That's what Matt wants. He thinks that if he pushes you away – you have no idea how much it hurts him to do it - you'll soon stop trying to befriend him, and everything will go back to the way it was before the flight. He'll continue to admire you from a distance, but there'd be no friendship.

"He couldn't stand to be asked any questions from you or anybody else about the flight and definitely would not want any recognition. The absolute worst sin you could commit would be to show him any gratitude.

"I don't like this option for Matt since he'd be returning to a miserable, isolated existence. It's one that he has learned to cope with, though, and as bad as it is, this is the option Matt is hoping for.

"The third option isn't really an option since it would never be approved, but one I think Matt is also considering: putting in for a transfer to another Group. I don't like this option because it would isolate Matt even further, and I think it would make him an even greater risk to himself. Luckily, the questions that Matt would have to answer from your CO, not to mention Doctor Garnett's intervention to block it – yes, he's the one that asked me to interview you two, knowing my progressive views, to see if I could discreetly help – eliminates this option.

"The fourth option is you could rescue him. I think if we teamed up on him, we'd be able to break through his defenses. But he'll be a tough sell: when it comes to you, he has no imagination

– he could never imagine you would want to be his friend, or more, out of anything but gratitude - and will fight you tooth and nail.

"He's so ashamed right now that he telegraphed his affection for you that he can't think straight. And I'm guessing he might have said something to you that he is even more ashamed of. Your opinion of him means everything to him; I think it would kill him if he thought you were disgusted by him.

"By the way, Matt would be terrified of this option if he was even able to conceive of it. But I like this option the best, at least for Matt.

"So, I need to know before I give away any more of Matt's secrets, what do you want to happen? This is a lot to lay on you. Just say the word, and I can make this problem go away, and you'll never have to deal with it again."

Jeff was shocked at how candid Captain Spiegel had been.

"The first option would be safe and might ease his father's mind, and if anything happens to Matt and I could have influenced your sending him home and didn't, I would never forgive myself.

But I'm selfish and want Matt here, with me. I think I can make him happy, and I know that would make his father happy, too.

"The second option is totally unacceptable. I couldn't stand to be around him and not be able to talk to him, let alone be friends with him. And there is no way I'm letting him go back to being alone, isolated.

"I want the fourth option more than I can say. I'm so miserable right now without him. Every time he pushes me away, I feel like my heart is being yanked out. I just don't know what to do. I've tried everything I can think of. If you're sure this is what he wants but just doesn't know it or thinks it's possible and that I wouldn't be forcing myself on him, then I'm begging you for your help."

Captain Spiegel was more than assured by Jeff's answer. But he didn't want Jeff to take on more than he was capable of.

"Jeff, I'm really glad you feel that way and know I'm pressing my luck, but I feel like I have to ask. You know what I'm suggesting, right? Have you thought this through? Are you able to do this without compromising yourself? Matt loves you the way you are, and he would not want you to do anything that would risk changing you."

"I love him, too. There is nothing remotely disgusting about that. If religion, psychiatry, teachers, my friends, and the Army say otherwise, they are all wrong. They can think what they want about me, but if my loving Matt is disgusting to them, screw them. I'd throw my parents and my brothers in, but I know they will love Matt as much as I do," then added, "Who in their right mind wouldn't?"

That was all Captain Spiegel needed to hear. He decided he'd help Jeff break through Matt's defenses.

"OK, Jeff. So, here's my advice on how to break through.

"Matt is good at lying, but only about his feelings. He's really a very honest person.

"First, ignore everything Matt says from more than six feet away. He's been practicing his defenses all his life, and he's way better at that distance than we'll ever be.

"He's been a busy beaver since the flight, building his walls sky-high, so you need to get him to come out from behind his walls and to come to you.

"He's got two major vulnerabilities. The first is he cares about you more than he cares about himself. He's already proven that a half dozen times; that's a given.

"The second is his defenses will quickly collapse when you're closer than six feet. By the time you get within three feet, his brain will already be short-circuiting. And by the time you've closed the distance and you're touching him, he'll only be capable of either silence or telling the truth.

"These insights will work only for you - because he cares so much about you - and are not transferable to anyone else, but they should work for you forever.

"You have a vulnerability, too, though. Luckily, Matt isn't aware of it yet, or he'd be using it to block you. You're hyper-protective of him, always were, and always will be. Don't let him know before your breakthrough, or you could be in big trouble.

Thomas Willard © 2021

Tell him afterward, though, because you'll need his help for your friendship to remain discreet.

"After his walls collapse, you can share these vulnerabilities, yours and his, with him. You should have no secrets from each other from now on. You need to impress this on Matt: he can hide or lie to anyone else, and you'll swear to whatever he says, but he can't hide from you anymore; you can't stand it. Tell him as soon as possible about everything that you did for him after he fell unconscious. I know you're modest, too, and probably think that you should spare him those details. But he needs to hear the details so he knows you're not acting out of gratitude. Learning them convinced me that you love him, and they should help convince him, too, though I'm sure, like me, he will be able to see it in your eyes."

Jeff absorbed all this information and then asked Captain Spiegel if he knew where Matt was right then. The Captain said he'd gone to the YMCA pool early that morning for a few hours when he could have the pool to himself. Jeff, reminded then that

Matt had lied to him about knowing how to swim, thought of a plan that would combine both of Matt's vulnerabilities if he only had the courage to go through with it.

Jeff asked if the Captain knew how to get to the Y, and the Captain said yes and that he'd be glad to drive him. The Captain asked if Jeff knew how to swim because he thought he'd heard somewhere that he didn't, but Jeff just smiled and said, "Not yet." Then he asked if the Captain would help arrange for Jeff to be alone with Matt in the pool, and the Captain said he would speak to the Y's manager. Jeff said great but warned that they should ignore any noise coming from the pool.

He then asked the Captain for one more favor. Could he arrange for Jeff to be moved into Matt's room? The Captain said he was sure of it.

On the short drive to town, Jeff began worrying that he and the Captain could be wrong, that Matt wasn't interested in Jeff that way. So, he asked Captain Spiegel what evidence he had that Matt loved him.

Thomas Willard © 2021

The Captain recounted how he had noticed Matt trembling the night before when he was speaking to Jeff. The Captain had thought Matt was either afraid of Jeff physically – ridiculous on its face – or of his emotional attachment to Jeff. He was betting heavily on the latter.

Then the Captain told Jeff how he had baited Matt and gotten the reaction he expected: Matt had become extremely defensive and protective of Jeff. To hear Matt tell the story, Jeff had flown the rescue mission. The Captain had gotten clear confirmation of Matt's love for Jeff, but it had come at a price: Matt hated him. He could live with that, though, if, in the end, he'd helped bring Matt and Jeff together.

#

NICE DIVE

They arrived at the YMCA and headed for the front desk. Captain Spiegel asked to see the manager, and the person behind the desk, a man in his mid-sixties, said that he was the manager and asked how he could help. The Captain pointed to Jeff and said they were from the Manor up the road and understood that visiting servicemen had been given guest privileges at the Y. The manager said that was correct and that all servicemen were welcome to use their facilities, including the pool. He had some loaner workout clothing and swimsuits they could use, and he could fix them up with a locker.

The Captain asked the manager to provide Jeff with a swimsuit and locker, and then pointed Jeff in the direction of the pool and locker room and said, "Good luck."

He waited for Jeff to get out of earshot, then turned to the manager to ask him for some additional help.

"I'm a visiting doctor at the Manor. There's another pilot already at the pool who's been coming here for the past few days. You might have noticed him, Matt Yetman. I understand he's an excellent swimmer and diver." The manager said he and the lifeguard had noticed Matt, who came early in the morning when

Thomas Willard © 2021

there were no other swimmers around. They'd been very impressed by his diving.

"Well, they're two of the best pilots in their Group, but they have some personal issues to work out between themselves. I know it's a lot to ask, but if there is no one else in the pool area, could you give them some privacy and pull the lifeguard out on some pretext for a few minutes? It's pretty important, or I wouldn't ask."

The manager said he understood and was young once himself. Then he picked up the phone, called the lifeguard, and asked him to come to the front desk and not to worry about leaving Matt alone in the pool.

When the lifeguard, a high school boy of about 16, arrived at the front desk, the manager told him the Captain was there on a special assignment and that Matt needed to practice something secret in the pool for a few minutes. Then, he asked the lifeguard to put on some of the loaner clothes - no need to go back to the locker room and change - and go to Cheswick's, the sandwich shop across the street, and get tea and crisps for the three of them, handing him a one-pound note.

The manager waited for the boy to grab a sweater and pair of trousers, quickly put them on over his swimsuit, and leave by the main door before turning to the Captain and saying, "That should give them at least a half-hour. No one is in there except for the two of them, and I can hold anyone else off who shows up for at least that long, telling them there's a maintenance issue with the pool."

The Captain was very appreciative and thought he owed the manager a warning, "There could be some yelling coming from the pool."

But the manager just nodded, saying, "I expect so. That's why it's good that the lifeguard, Tim, won't be here to hear it."

Jeff found his locker and quickly changed into his swimsuit. Not familiar with pool procedures, he didn't shower but grabbed a towel and headed for the pool.

He could hear the water lapping as he neared the door to the pool, and he paused there for a moment. The door had a window, and he could see Matt on the diving board. Matt took three steps to the end of the board, jumped, and landed on the end of the board, sprung into the air, did a somersault, and then straightened as he smoothly dove into the water headfirst, barely making a ripple. He swam the length of the pool underwater and surfaced about two feet from the shallow end.

Jeff, shaking a little, barged through the door, all smiles, and said, "Hi, Matt, nice dive," then added with a slightly challenging edge to his voice, "I thought you couldn't swim."

Matt, thinking he was alone and now shocked to find Jeff standing there, just said, "Thanks. What are you doing here?"

Jeff made his pitch.

"I have a favor to ask. I'm petrified of the water, but I want you to teach me how to swim. You're the only one I trust. We fly over the Channel every day, and I should know how to swim. My family is very worried about me but would worry less if they knew I could swim.

"I'll make a bargain with you: you teach me how to swim, and I'll teach you how to dance. I think you're as terrified of dancing as I am of swimming, so it'd be a fair trade."

Matt, knowing it would be impossible for him to teach Jeff to swim – he couldn't be in the water, holding him, nearly naked, without embarrassing himself - just looked down and said, "I can't," but started to add "but the Y has a great program, and you have all week…", but Jeff cut him off, saying,

"I'll only trust you. Why can't you teach me?"

Matt could only answer, "I can't. I'm sorry, I just can't."

Jeff, knowing that would be Matt's answer, said, "OK, fine," walked to the deep end of the pool, and jumped in feet-first.

Matt watched in horror, then started screaming for help before diving down himself to try to rescue Jeff.

Thomas Willard © 2021

Jeff, literally in over his head and panicked, was near the bottom of the twelve-foot-deep pool, screaming underwater, losing all the air in his lungs and sucking in water in the process.

In an instant, Matt found Jeff and, despite Jeff's wild thrashing, managed to grab him around the waist and drag him to the shallow end of the pool. By then, Jeff seemed to be unconscious. Matt somehow found the strength to push Jeff out of the pool, climbed out himself, knelt beside him, and started giving him mouth-to-mouth resuscitation. Almost immediately, but after coughing up a mouthful of water, Jeff began to breathe on his own.

Matt, frantic, holding Jeff in his arms, called out to him, "Jeff, can you hear me?"

Jeff opened his eyes, looked at Matt, and asked in a hoarse voice, "Are you going to teach me to swim or not?"

Matt, seeing that Jeff was out of danger and maybe had never been unconscious, could only think of one thing to say. "I hate you."

Thomas Willard © 2021

Jeff just smiled and said, "No, you don't. You already told me you love me." Then Jeff asked again, "Are you going to teach me how to swim?"

Matt looked away and, in a whisper, said, "I can't. Please don't ask me why."

But Jeff already knew why. He could see the reason tenting Matt's swimsuit. So, he reached over and grabbed Matt's erection, asking, "Is this why?"

Matt, who hadn't been aware of his erection and was somehow incapable of lying to Jeff about it, was certain now that Jeff knew his secret. So, he covered his eyes with the crook of his arm, feeling shame beyond measure, and then waited for Jeff to register his disgust.

But Jeff had no intention of registering anything but his own love for Matt.

"Matt, give me your hand." But Matt couldn't move. "Let me get this straight. You can't teach me how to swim because you care for me too much?"

Thomas Willard © 2021

Jeff gently took Matt's hand and placed it on his own erection while leaving his hand on Matt's. Matt, in disbelief, lowered his arm from his eyes and turned his head to look at Jeff.

Jeff softly said, "I love you, too," then, grinning from ear to ear, asked, "Now, can you teach me how to swim?"

The lifeguard had just returned with the tea, earlier than expected, when he heard Matt's cries for help from the pool. But the manager stopped him from responding with a wave of his hand, signaling he should take a seat, then calmly asked the Captain if he took milk or lemon with his tea. After several minutes, the Captain could no longer stand the suspense and excused himself to look through the pool's outer-door window. He saw Matt and Jeff out of the water, lying together on the deck at the shallow end of the pool, wrapped in each other's arms.

#

SWIMMING LESSON

Captain Spiegel returned to the front desk and gave the manager a smile and a thumbs-up. He thanked the manager again and said that the coast was clear, he could send the lifeguard back, but asked if the manager would phone the pool first to give Matt a heads-up: he wouldn't want the lifeguard to walk in on Matt practicing any secret judo moves.

He let the lifeguard know that Matt was going to be teaching another pilot, Jeff, how to swim – nothing secret - but to just let them be, not pay them any attention.

He asked the lifeguard to let Jeff know that the Captain had driven back to the Manor – he had to see the staff manager about something - and hoped to meet them both there later at supper. Then the Captain shook the manager's hand, each nodding knowingly to the other, and left.

Matt and Jeff were still holding each other when the pool phone rang. They quickly separated themselves, moved to the edge of the pool, and sat with their legs dangling in the water just before

Thomas Willard © 2021

the lifeguard entered, who waved to them and then came over to give Jeff the Captain's message.

After the lifeguard had left to take up his station overseeing the pool, Matt asked Jeff,

"Why was Captain Spiegel here? How did you find me?"

"Matt, Captain Spiegel is helping us. He's way smarter than the two of us combined and figured everything out. I think Doc Garnett knows, too. I sort of had a meltdown in the ambulance, and the Doc asked Captain Spiegel, who is some kind of expert in combat fatigue, to check us out, though I think they both knew it wasn't combat fatigue.

"Captain Spiegel is what you'd call unconventional, which is why I think Doc Garnett chose him. He interviewed me this morning and didn't beat around the bush.

"He took a big chance in telling me his theory of why you were avoiding me and checked to see what I wanted to do about it if anything. When I told him that I was desperate, at the end of my rope, that I loved you, and either you weren't interested or were pushing me away for another reason that I couldn't figure out, he offered to help.

"He told me how to get past your defenses, that you had two vulnerabilities we could exploit: you cared about me more than yourself, and that your defenses would collapse if I got within touching distance," then Jeff proudly added, "I came up with the rest of the plan myself."

Matt, feeling overwhelmed but not wanting to break down in public, just said, "He spoke to me last night, and I gave him a really hard time. He probably thinks I hate him."

"Yeah, he definitely got that impression. It's OK, Matt. He said he deserved it. He feels really bad about having to bait you, but it was the only way he could think of to know for sure what was bothering you; you certainly weren't going to tell him, and I didn't have a clue. And this is kind of touchy stuff.

"It's OK, don't feel bad, he understands. He won't let you apologize since he knows he purposely provoked you, but maybe you could just thank him when we see him later.

Despite being asked not to, the lifeguard was watching Matt and Jeff like a hawk, hoping to pick up some secret judo moves from Matt. Jeff noticed and said, "Maybe we should talk about this later when we're in private."

Matt agreed, then said, "You ready for your first lesson?"

Jeff, now confronted with the realization he was going to have to go back in the water, tried to stall, "Maybe we could wait until tomorrow?"

Matt, who realized the baton had been passed to him and it was now his turn to lead, said, "No, it'll be fun, I promise. I've got you; you're safe, trust me." Matt didn't need to say it, though; Jeff already did.

Jeff asked Matt to go in first and to swim for him to show him how to do it. Not thinking Jeff was stalling any longer, Matt lowered himself into the water, dove under, and swam to the far side. He surfaced, then swam back using the freestyle or front crawl stroke. When he reached the side near Jeff, he did a smooth turn and then did a backstroke to the far side before doing another turn and using the breaststroke to wind up back in front of Jeff.

Standing in the 3-foot-deep water in front of Jeff, Matt said, "See, easy. Even I can do it." Then he climbed the ladder just beside Jeff and got out to join him by the edge.

"Matt, that was amazing. You're like a fish in the water. And you seem so natural and confident in there, the happiest I've ever seen you."

Matt replied, "I grew up across the street from Fishermans Beach, in Swampscott, about twelve miles north of Boston. All of us kids learned to swim by about three, so I guess it is natural to me. But it's not hard to learn. I promise. And you don't need to know much to be safe around water.

"I know you're terrified. I won't tease you, no horsing around."

Jeff asked, "OK, how do we start? Do I get a float?"

Thomas Willard © 2021

Matt answered, "No, not yet; we're not going past the three-foot mark today. I'll be your float, and you can ride on my back."

Jeff smiled and said, "Well, if you'd told me that, I would have been in the water ten minutes ago just for the chance to grope you."

Matt stood up and took Jeff's hand to help him up but also to do a little groping of his own. Then he walked Jeff to the ladder and said that he'd go down first, one rung at a time, to show Jeff how to back down the ladder, and that Jeff should follow, keeping pace with Matt, and that Matt would keep a hand centered on Jeff's back all the way down; Jeff needed to use both hands to hold the rails of the ladder all the way down.

They both made it safely down the ladder, but Matt noticed by the last rung Jeff was shaking. Matt told Jeff to stay where he was and to hold on to the ladder with both hands. Then Matt moved away from Jeff and searched for the drop-off point, the edge of the three-foot-deep section of the pool, also marked on the pool deck and sides, with his foot. He showed Jeff where the edge was, eight feet from the shallow end of the pool, and promised they would not go near the edge that day. Then he moved back to Jeff and sat down on the pool bottom. With his head still sticking out of the water, Matt said, "See, I'm sitting on the bottom and can still breathe." Then he sprung up out of the water to stand.

He went back to Jeff and said, "We're just going to walk from one side of the pool to the other, staying well within the 3-foot-deep zone, and you're going to hold onto me the whole way."

Matt thought he might have to pry Jeff's hands from the ladder's rails, but when he took one of Jeff's hands and placed it on his own waist, Jeff's other hand quickly followed. Matt waited for a moment and then started walking to the opposite side of the pool. When they got there, Jeff's shaking seemed to have lessened, and after waiting a moment, they started back.

They traversed the pool about five times before Jeff's shaking stopped. So, Matt thought he'd try the next step. He brought Jeff back to the ladder, then knelt and swam around close by, using a doggy-paddle type stroke. Then he positioned himself half-submerged at Jeff's feet and asked, "Ready for a ride?" When Jeff didn't move, he added, "Groping is allowed."

Jeff, whose shaking had resumed, immediately let go of the ladder and climbed onto Matt's back. Matt told him to grab him around the neck and not to let go, but that if he did fall off, to just stand up. When Jeff seemed ready, Matt started for the far side of the pool, being sure to keep his and Jeff's head above water.

When they reached the far side, Matt asked Jeff to stand while he turned around and, once turned, asked Jeff to climb back on. Then Matt swam to the opposite side of the pool.

By the fourth traverse, Jeff had stopped shaking and was thoroughly enjoying himself. He loved being this close to Matt, with Matt in his element. And he loved how Matt was so confident but, at the same time, so tender. He really liked seeing Matt this way.

Matt could sense that Jeff was feeling more relaxed, even randy: he'd groped Matt more than once without hiding his intention. So, he suggested they try the next step: swimming underwater but still together, with Jeff on his back.

Jeff was having such a good time that he didn't want to stop but understood that there was more to learning how to swim than groping your instructor. So, he said, sure, he was game.

Matt had Jeff stand up and noticed Jeff didn't immediately lunge for the ladder's rails, which he took as a good sign. So, Matt again sat on the bottom, but this time, he had Jeff sit next to him. Matt realized by now that the more body contact there was between them, the better, so he deliberately sat so that their shoulders and thighs touched. The result was no shaking by Jeff.

He had Jeff place his hands on the bottom of the pool, then told Jeff they were just going to duck their heads underwater and immediately pull them back out. He'd show Jeff how to do it first.

Matt exaggerated holding his breath, quickly ducked his head underwater, then pulled it back out and loudly exhaled. He did this twice more, then asked Jeff to do it with him, which Jeff did surprisingly well. After repeating that a half dozen times, Matt

Thomas Willard © 2021

said they were going to do the same thing but count to ten before pulling their head out. They did that about four or five times, and then Matt increased the hold time to thirty seconds. When they finished doing that, Matt figured they were ready for the next step.

He crouched down again and asked Jeff to get on his back. He told him that, in a moment, they were going to swim underwater to the far side of the pool - much less than thirty seconds away. But first, he wanted them to practice synchronizing holding their breaths. When Matt said, "Go," Jeff was to hold his breath until Matt stood up.

Jeff said he was ready. Matt counted down, "Three, two, one. Go!" and ducked down as Jeff held his breath. Matt counted to five to himself and stood up, forcing Jeff off his back and onto his feet.

They practiced this one more time, and Matt thought they were ready. Matt told Jeff that if at any point he was uncomfortable, he should just let go of Matt's neck and stand up.

Thomas Willard © 2021

Matt counted down, "Three, two, one. Go!" then dove

under the water and swam for the far side of the pool. He felt Jeff

on his back all the way and climb off as Matt stood up.

Jeff was beside himself, "That was so great!" and hugged

Matt, who was sure he could get used to that.

They traversed the pool several times, with an exuberant

Jeff hugging Matt each time. Finally, Matt was getting tired and

thought they should finish soon. But he wanted to try one more

step. He wanted Jeff to try swimming underwater on his own.

"Jeff, you've been doing amazing. I'm having a great time.

Do you think you can handle one more step before we call it quits

for today?"

Jeff couldn't think anything could be better than what

they'd been doing, but it seemed important to Matt to reach a

certain goal for the first lesson, so he said he was ready to try.

Matt got Jeff to stand next to him, facing the far side of the

pool. He showed Jeff how to first hold his breath, then dive

forward, and then open his eyes underwater. He had Jeff watch

Thomas Willard © 2021

how Matt used his arms to pull himself forward underwater – he'd worry about kicking later - and to combine the steps: holding his breath, diving forward, and pulling himself forward with his arms. They were ready.

Matt had Jeff stand to the side of him, the side the farthest away from the drop-off edge. Then he asked if Jeff was ready. Jeff nodded he was, and Matt counted down, "Three, two, one. Go!" and delayed diving forward an instant so that Jeff could dive first.

Jeff dove forward head-first, and though he was barely below the water's surface, he felt like he was twenty feet below. His heart was pounding, and he was swimming in every direction, but when he opened his eyes, he saw Matt right there next to him, giving him a thumbs-up and an occasional bump to keep him away from the deep end.

When Jeff reached the far side of the pool twenty seconds later, he stood up. But this time, it was Matt who was the exuberant one. He was hugging Jeff in the tightest embrace Jeff could ever remember and making so much noise in the echo chamber of the

Thomas Willard © 2021

pool that it was embarrassing. But when Jeff looked back at how far he'd just swam on his own underwater, he felt an immense sense of accomplishment - for fighting through his fear – and relief, all due to the screaming guy next to him.

There was another ladder on that side of the pool, and they used it to exit the pool, Jeff first, with Matt following closely behind, keeping a reassuring hand on Jeff's back.

When Jeff looked at the pool, he was no longer terrified by it. There were only good memories associated with it now: of Matt diving, of holding Matt, even of groping Matt in and out of the pool, and of his underwater swim across it. He knew Matt would never have a problem talking him into going to the pool again; in fact, he couldn't wait for his next lesson.

For Matt, today wasn't about giving Jeff a swimming lesson; it was about getting Jeff over being terrified of the water, and it seemed he now was. Matt had over a week to teach Jeff how to swim, which should be more than enough time. Matt looked at the diving board and thought, "For sure, come Graduation Day."

Thomas Willard © 2021

They waved goodbye to the lifeguard, who was convinced by then he'd learned enough karate and judo watching Matt that he could get a job with MI5, and headed for the locker room. Their lockers were not near to each other, and by the time Matt had removed his swimsuit, wrapped a towel around his waist, and was heading for the showers, he was feeling a little shy again.

Jeff was already in the shower and expected Matt to join him. But when Matt came into the shower room, he picked the shower head the farthest from Jeff instead. Jeff knew what was bothering Matt by then and realized it was his turn to take charge and help Matt get over his fears. But not here. He'd wait until they got back to the Manor. He had another plan, well, really the continuation of his first plan. Jeff thought, "Live it up shy, ashamed-Matt. Like the song says, "There'll Be Some Changes Made," and very soon.

#

DANCING LESSON

Thomas Willard © 2021

Once they finished dressing and put their towels and swimsuits in the laundry basket, Matt and Jeff walked to the front desk and handed in their locker keys. They thanked the manager and asked if there was a place handy where they could grab a sandwich. The manager directed them to Cheswick's, the tea and sandwich shop across the street, and told them to come back anytime.

It was only 1115, still early for lunch, so the sandwich shop was nearly empty, and they grabbed a booth normally meant for four. They ordered some ham and cheese sandwiches and tea and chatted while their meal was being prepared. Jeff noticed that Matt wasn't as shy, would speak to him, and respond to any questions, but was more comfortable listening to Jeff talk.

At one point, Jeff noticed Matt staring at him, and when Matt realized he'd been caught, he blushed and then fell silent. Jeff knew what to do. He stretched his leg out and brushed against one of Matt's, who instantly moved his leg away. But when Jeff followed Matt's leg with his own, Matt left his leg there and allowed the contact.

Thomas Willard © 2021

Then, Jeff nonchalantly moved his leg just enough to let Matt know he was deliberately touching him. Though Matt continued to blush, he resumed speaking. From then on, Jeff used any excuse to reach over and touch Matt, his arm and shoulder, even touching his hands to make a point.

Eventually, he got Matt to relax enough to contribute to the conversation. At one point, when Matt had brought up his love of sailing, he seemed totally relaxed. Jeff, who knew nothing about sailing, just smiled contentedly: he could listen to an enthusiastic Matt talk like this forever.

They finished their meal, then started the two-mile walk back to the Manor. It was a beautiful, warm spring day, and there was little or no traffic on the narrow country road, most of which was lined with six-foot-tall hedges. Jeff, not wanting to risk Matt withdrawing again, kept his arm over Matt's shoulder, pulling him in close, and quickly steered the conversation back to swimming or sailing if there seemed to be an awkward lull developing.

Thomas Willard © 2021

When they got to the Manor, one of the staff told Jeff he had a note from Captain Spiegel waiting for him at the front desk. Matt told Jeff he was going to take a shower – he'd only rinsed himself at the Y – and he'd see him later. When Jeff looked at him with a questioning expression, Matt said, "For sure this time, no lie," and then climbed the stairs to his room.

Jeff went to the front desk and asked if they had a note for him. The desk manager handed Jeff the note, which read,

Dear Jeff,

Something's come up, and I've been called back to the hospital for a few days. I'll try to get back on Friday, though, to check to see how you guys are doing.

I'm sorry for invading your privacy, but I stole a look at you guys when you were out of the pool – from all the yelling, I had to see if you'd drowned each other.

I only looked for a second, but I was very happy at what I saw, and I'd say your plan definitely worked. I had some idea of

what you were going to do, but wow, are you nuts! (I'm just asking as an astonished layman, not professionally).

Your room has been changed to share with Matt; they've already moved your stuff. I've guessed you have another plan up your sleeve but that you may at some point doubt yourself and worry that you're forcing Matt into something he isn't ready for or, worse, doesn't want. To help ease your mind, I'll tell you what I saw when I looked through the window.

You and Matt are pretty much alike, the same height and build. I saw you two guys embracing each other, but from my vantage point, you were indistinguishable - I couldn't tell who was who. Your embrace was mutual, though, or I would have assumed you were leading the charge: Matt was holding you as tightly as you were holding him, or I could have recognized you by the difference.

You're not forcing Matt into anything; I told you before he has a lack of imagination when it comes to you. He's put you on a pedestal and can't conceive of you "wanting" him. You might have got him to accept that you love him - as a brother or best friend -

and that maybe you even enjoyed some physical contact, but his

doubts about you "wanting" him started to return the second you

separated at the pool.

At this point, Matt is probably the happiest he's been in his

whole life. Someone he cares about has discovered his secret and

still accepts him. He won't risk anything that could destroy that, so

he's going to suppress any romantic feelings he has for you.

You could leave things as they are: you've already done

Matt an amazing amount of good. You could be friends, very close

friends, when you return to base. And I have no worries that Matt

is any longer a risk to himself.

But if you want things to develop further, you'll have to

make the first move. And you'll have no better opportunity than

now, at the Manor.

No matter what you decide to do, I'll always be there to

help.

Thomas Willard © 2021

Good luck with your plan (I can't imagine what you have in store for him this time; let the yelling begin)!

Yours, John

P.S. To put the "gratitude issue" to bed forever before it has a chance to undermine your progress with him, you need to tell Matt as soon as possible everything you did to save him, from when the plane first touched down, your threatening to kill yourself to extort his transfusion in the ambulance, all your scheming to get to visit him in the hospital, and, your vigil at his bedside and help in getting him to regain consciousness. Don't spare him any details: they will convince him of your love for him, as they did me. If, when you finish, he's still being obstinate, tell him I said nobody in my entire professional experience has ever been that grateful. Devoted; yes, though you take the cake on that score. Grateful; no.

Jeff confirmed that his room had been changed, then looked around for one of the Red Cross staff women. He saw one in the main lounge area and approached her to ask a favor. Could he borrow the portable record player for a few hours and a couple of records? He wanted to take it to his room to teach his roommate how to dance. He said he knew the Red Cross women would be glad to teach his roommate - that's pretty much what they were there for - but that his roommate was terrified of dancing, and he just wanted to help him get over the hump in private. He said once his roommate was able to move at all, they were welcome to him, but that they needed to be gentle with him and to only dance slow songs.

The woman said he was welcome to borrow the record player and that no one would be looking for it until at least tea time. And she said she'd look to Jeff for a signal when his roommate could be approached and asked to dance.

Jeff selected two records, gathered up the record player, and waited for Matt, whose door could be seen from the lobby, to return from the shower.

Matt, not wanting to use all the hot water, quickly showered. He had just returned to his room when he heard a single

Thomas Willard © 2021

knock, sounding more like a kick, at the door. He opened it to find Jeff with his hands full, holding a record player.

"Hey Matt, looks like we're roommates. Where can I put this?"

Matt had noticed his bed had been changed and new, clean civilian clothes laid out on the two twin beds in the room. He'd thought the staff had forgotten their promise to move him into a single and assumed they were giving him a new roommate but didn't care. Now, he was excited to find Jeff was his new roommate.

"Wow, we're roomies; that's great. You can plop that thing down anywhere, maybe one of the beds."

Jeff spied the electrical outlet near the nightstand between the two beds and motioned for Matt to clear it off. Matt did, and then Jeff set the player down and plugged it in.

Matt thought, "Great, Jeff loves music. Now we'll have something to listen to," but Jeff had other plans.

"Matt, remember our deal. You teach me to swim; I teach you to dance. Well, it's pay-back time."

Matt, just wearing a bathrobe and a towel wrapped around his waist, was scared stiff: Jeff wanted to teach him to dance right there, right then. He tried to stall, "Ah, I'm a little tired. Maybe we could do this tomorrow?"

But Jeff knew that if he left things up to Matt, tomorrow would never come, so he just ignored Matt and continued setting up the player, loading the two records onto the record changer.

Then, before Matt got the idea to put on some clothes, Jeff started peeling his off, saying, "It's too hot in here for this."

By the time he'd gotten down to just his boxers and t-shirt, an obviously frightened Matt was visibly shaking.

"Come on, Matt, it'll be fine. I only brought two songs, so this will just take five minutes. I promise I've got you, trust me."

Matt was worried he couldn't trust himself. Everything was going great with Jeff; he didn't want to ruin it. But Jeff seemed

Thomas Willard © 2021

determined to get Matt to dance with him, as determined as Matt had been to get Jeff into the pool.

Matt thought maybe he could contain himself and not react; it was only five minutes. But then Jeff said, "You won't be needing this," and pulled Matt's bathrobe off, tossing it to Jeff's bed.

Matt was trembling now, so Jeff lifted his t-shirt off and pulled it down over Matt, saying, "Here, you're shivering," then rubbed Matt's back to comfort and warm him.

Then Jeff explained to Matt what they were about to do.

"Today, we're only going to dance to two slow songs. They're easy; even I can do them."

That got Matt to smile a little, remembering it was the same phrase he'd used to get Jeff back in the pool.

"This first song, Billie Holiday's great version of "I'll Be Seeing You," is the slowest song I know, almost a dirge.

"You just put your arms around my neck, like I did when I was swimming on your back, and move with me.OK, you ready?"

Thomas Willard © 2021

Matt nodded yes but then added in a quivering voice, "I don't think I can talk anymore."

Jeff said, "That's all right, I'll do all the talking," and hit play.

Jeff moved close to Matt. Matt put his arms around Jeff's neck, while Jeff put his arms around Matt's waist just as the record started.

Though Matt had his arms around Jeff, he kept himself separated from Jeff by about a foot and wasn't moving. Jeff started swaying back and forth and used his hands on Matt's waist to guide him.

Matt started to sway a little but kept himself at arms-length. The record was half over, and the first goal in Jeff's plan hadn't been met – he wanted Matt in intimate contact with him – so Jeff moved his arms around Matt's waist and started applying pressure to move Matt closer, saying every few seconds, "That's it. You're doing good."

Thomas Willard © 2021

At first, Matt didn't realize the gap between him and Jeff had closed – he was concentrating on keeping himself in check. But when first his hip and then his groin touched Jeff's, Matt panicked and tried to pull away. Jeff had already tightened his hold, though, so all Matt could do was rub himself into Jeff, which made things worse. Matt quickly lost his battle and was fully erect as the song ended.

Matt felt mortified and managed to mumble, "I'm so ashamed," but Jeff, encouraged that Matt hadn't bolted for the door, tried to comfort him, saying, "What's there to be ashamed of? Yeah, I can feel you; can't you feel me? I think we're the same size - everywhere."

Jeff told Matt the next song was Bing Crosby and Les Paul's version of "It's Been A Long Time."

As the changer dropped the record and the song began, Jeff pulled Matt even closer and said, "Slow dancing isn't about fancy footwork. It's all about body contact," and he started to sway in an exaggerated way, rubbing his groin across Matt's.

Thomas Willard © 2021

It didn't take Matt long to start squirming. He was holding a nearly naked Jeff in his arms; their groins were rubbing, and he was quickly losing control. He had to separate his middle from Jeff's before he embarrassed himself: the shame of it would be unbearable.

Jeff, who could feel Matt's increasingly desperate attempts to separate himself, kept his exaggerated swaying, rubbing Matt's back, soothingly saying, "You're doing good. The song's almost over. I've got you."

Matt thought Jeff didn't understand what was about to happen. Matt couldn't speak - he felt his whole body betraying him. Finally, with just ten seconds of the song remaining, Matt managed to say, to try to stop himself, "No!" but it was too late.

When Matt said "No," Jeff instinctively released his hold but then quickly reapplied it just as Matt began to convulse in his arms. Jeff thought, "That's it, Matt. Just let it go," and continued to hold him as he felt Matt's knees buckle.

Thomas Willard © 2021

Jeff rubbed Matt's back and said, "There, that's dancing. You did great! That wasn't so bad, right?" And then gently kissed Matt on the cheek.

It took a few moments for Matt, who'd covered his eyes again with the crook of his arm, to reply. "I'm sorry. I'm so disgusting."

Jeff tried to pry Matt's arm away, saying, "Matt, look at me. I promise, the last thing you'll see on my face is disgust," but Matt wouldn't move.

So, Jeff repeated what he'd done at the pool, saying, "Matt, give me your hand."

When Matt didn't offer his hand, Jeff gently took it and placed it on his own stomach. Then, he dragged Matt's hand down past his waistband and onto his own semen-soaked boxers covering his erection, saying, "I think we were disgusting at about the same time."

Then, Jeff released Matt for a moment to turn Matt's bed down. He embraced Matt again and said, "Dancing always wears me out. I usually need a nap after. That was your first time, so you must be exhausted," and then guided Matt, who was still covering his eyes with his arm, onto the bed.

Before lying Matt down, Jeff said, "You're not shaking anymore. Can I have my t-shirt back?" and without waiting for a reply, gently lifted his t-shirt off of Matt.

Matt was lying on his back and expected Jeff to leave, but instead, Jeff climbed into bed with him, saying, "Hey, you're hogging the bed. Could you move over a little?"

Jeff lifted his butt off the bed and removed his boxers, saying, "Yuk, I'm making a mess of your nice clean sheets," before tossing his boxers to the floor. Then, before Matt could protest, Jeff pulled the towel off Matt, belatedly asking, "Can I borrow your towel?" and wiped himself dry.

Jeff shocked Matt even further by using the other end of the towel to wipe Matt dry, even gently holding Matt's penis to dry that too. As he finished, in a loving voice, Jeff said, "There you go, good as new." Then, he placed the towel at the foot of the bed.

Looking at Matt lying naked before him, Jeff said, "There is nothing disgusting about you. To me, you're perfect, and your body is a thing of beauty. You couldn't be disgusting to me if you tried."

Jeff laid on his back, but before pulling the covers over them, he thought he needed to offer himself to Matt. "I think we need to keep things even, or you'll go "I'm so disgusting" on me again. I looked at and touched you, so it's your turn to do the same to me - fair's fair - but you're better looking than me, so I guess it won't be a completely fair trade after all."

Jeff waited for Matt to take him up on his offer, but when Matt didn't move, Jeff's doubts flooded back. He and Captain Spiegel had gotten everything wrong; Matt had no interest in him like that. Matt had said no and tried to pull away. He'd forced himself on Matt - molested him.

Now, it was Jeff who was covering his eyes with the crook of his arm.

Thomas Willard © 2021

"Oh, God, I'm so sorry, Matt. I totally misread everything. You told me no, but I kept forcing myself on you. I guess I wanted you to like me like that so much that I ignored what you were saying.

"For some reason, I can't move; just give me a second. I'll go ask to have my room changed again. I promise you won't see me the rest of the time we're here. I'm so sorry, I'm really so…" but then Jeff felt a hand softly land on his chest.

Matt moved his hand to gently rub Jeff's chest, then slowly moved it down to rub his stomach before moving it further down to rub Jeff's groin. In an almost reverent way, he lifted Jeff's penis and held it in his hand for a moment before gently lowering it to Jeff's groin. Then he moved his hand back to Jeff's stomach, patted it three times, and then rubbed it twice to signal his appreciation for Jeff's body.

Matt tried to gently pry Jeff's arm from his eyes, but when that failed, and determined to show Jeff how much he loved him, he tried another tactic. He kissed Jeff on his forehead, then on the

Thomas Willard © 2021

top of his head. Then he kissed him on any exposed area of Jeff's face he could reach. But when all that failed, Matt laid between Jeff's legs and, with their chests touching, playfully simulated grinding their two groins together. That did the trick.

Jeff removed his arm covering his eyes, opened them, and smiled at Matt, asking,

"Keeping things even?"

Matt, his senses still overwhelmed and unable to speak, could only nod yes.

Then Matt rolled off to Jeff's side, keeping one leg draped over Jeff's and his erection on top of Jeff's leg, no longer ashamed to show his arousal. He placed his hand on top of Jeff's head and began gently stroking his hair. His other arm lay across Jeff's chest, holding Jeff in a tight embrace. A tear ran down his face. He would remember these few moments forever as the best of his life.

#

THE ARRANGEMENT

Thomas Willard © 2021

Jeff had dozed off for about twenty minutes. When he started to wake, he could feel that Matt's arm was still around him, and he felt more relaxed than he had in a long time. But as Jeff started to show signs of waking, Matt tried to surreptitiously remove his arm, not sure he any longer had the right to hold him.

When Jeff opened his eyes, he found Matt staring back and then felt him quickly try to remove his arm. Before he could, Jeff locked Matt's arm with his own and said, half-menacingly, "Oh no, you don't. You better keep it there if you know what's good for you. We're not going through that again." Then he pulled him in tight to emphasize the point.

Jeff knew from what Captain Spiegel had told him that Matt would behave this way, constantly backslide, be insecure about Jeff's motives, and think that Jeff was only showing affection out of compassion or, worse, gratitude. So, he needed to convince Matt otherwise and knew he only had a short amount of time to do it. He turned to face Matt and held him close.

Thomas Willard © 2021

"We have to get one thing straight. You can hide your feelings from other people, but not from me, not anymore. I can't stand it; it hurts too much.

"Captain Spiegel, who knows us better than we know ourselves, told me you'd be a tough sell, that I'd have to pull out all the stops. He asked me to go over what happened just after the flight, things you missed while you were unconscious. When I finished, he made me promise that I'd tell you what I told him.

"I wanted to spare you these details, but he said it was important, that you wouldn't trust me completely if I didn't. So that you don't think this is all about gratitude or me just being a nice guy, here goes.

"You saved my life at least three times that day, but it looks like I might have saved yours just as many."

Then Jeff told Matt everything he did to try to save him after he passed out, from insisting on being removed immediately, ignoring calls for him to take the first ambulance, inviting Wes to ride along, his threat of killing himself to extort a direct transfusion

Thomas Willard © 2021

between him and Matt, of his scheming in the hospital to locate and visit Matt, of his first breakdown at Matt's bedside and rescue by the nurse, of his reading Matt's letter from his Dad over and over until he broke down a second time, and then the miracle of Matt's regaining consciousness.

Remembering these events caused Jeff to start to lose control, but he managed to keep himself together enough to blurt out his final, and hopefully, trump card, "And Captain Spiegel says if you still don't believe me, you're just being obstinate," which was not exactly an accurate quote.

In the middle of Jeff's recounting of events, Matt sensed Jeff struggling with his emotions and began stroking his hair again to try to comfort him. Matt had guessed some of what Jeff told him but had no idea the lengths that Jeff had gone to save him. Captain Spiegel was right; if he didn't believe Jeff now, he was just obstinate. He was so grateful to Jeff at that moment and loved him even more, then realized you could be grateful to someone and still love them. He'd never doubt Jeff's love for him again.

Thomas Willard © 2021

To let Jeff know that Matt's days of being obstinate were over, he gently kissed Jeff on the cheek, then said, "Thank you for everything you did and for telling me." Then, to lighten the mood a little, he asked,

"You gave me blood?" then gushed, "That's unbelievably great, makes us blood-brothers! I always wanted a brother."

Jeff sensed a change in Matt but had to be certain.

"You promise: no backsliding? And you'll tell me if anything is bothering you, no hiding? I'm getting better at reading you, so it won't be as easy for you to hide, but I'm no Captain Spiegel."

Matt said, "I promise. I never want to hurt you again."

Now that Jeff knew Matt accepted that he truly loved him, Jeff tried to allay Matt's other fears.

"Captain Spiegel said you're terrified of returning to the base, that you're considering a transfer. You think you've telegraphed your feelings to everyone by rescuing me. He also said you don't trust your motives for doing it; that you're no hero: if you had it to do over again, you probably wouldn't do it. Captain Spiegel told me, "Spoken like a true hero."

"First, everyone in the squadron, especially Colonel Jenkins, wants you back. If you think you telegraphed how you feel about me, you didn't. I heard the last thing you said before passing out, but I never assumed or flattered that you were talking about me. The only other person who knows is Captain Spiegel, and he'll take it to his grave.

"Everyone knows how modest you are and that you don't want to be asked anything about the flight or want any recognition. So, I've thought up an arrangement, and I promise I can get everyone to agree to its terms. You know me by now; I'm good at this kind of thing.

"No one will ever ask you or me anything about the flight. You won't suddenly become the most popular guy in the Officer's Club, and no one's going to remark on your amazing flying skills.

"But you have to do something for them. You have to hang out a little with them. It's ok to remain a bit of a wallflower; no one's going to force you to be the center of attention. When you feel comfortable, play a game of darts with one of them or me.

"I'll always be there to enforce the rules, but you'll have to be quick to rescue me with your magic touch if I'm about to make a fool of myself - Captain Spiegel said I always was, and always will be, hyper-protective of you. None of the other guys will fault me if I overreact, though.

"But in exchange, you'll have to do something for them: let them buy you a beer, the first one every night; it will be waiting for you at the bar. They'll rotate the privilege without fanfare. You'll never know whose turn it was that night. Just slightly raise your glass in acknowledgment in the direction of the largest group of guys. Everyone will pretend not to notice.

"Knowing the Colonel, he already has plans for you. He needs flight leaders, and if he has any say, you're going to be one. They would have broken our flight up anyway, worried one of us would repeat a rescue if the other was in trouble. But he knows we're too responsible for us to abandon a flight we are leading to save the other and risk the squadron or the mission.

"We're fighter pilots; we know the odds: a third of us or more won't survive the war. I'm not looking that far ahead. I'd be devastated if anything happened to you, and I guess you'd feel the same about me. But if it happened to either of us in combat, eventually, I think we'd come to grips with it. If something else happened to you, though, out of despair, I couldn't handle it. It would destroy me.

"If I'm asking too much and you just can't go back to the base, then let Captain Spiegel know, and he'll get you transferred or sent home. I don't want to lose you to despair. But if you think you could take a chance with me, with the other guys, I swear I'll do everything I can to make you comfortable."

Jeff said all this without looking at Matt. He was afraid that if he looked before he finished, he'd read there was no hope on Matt's face, and he'd never get all the way through. When he finally dared to look at Matt, he wasn't sure what he saw.

Thomas Willard © 2021

Matt had listened to Jeff pour his heart out, eliminating all his objections one by one. He had to admit, Captain Spiegel and now Jeff knew him well.

Matt hadn't said much for almost an hour. He looked Jeff in the eyes and said, "I've run out of excuses. I don't understand why you'd want to, but I accept you do love me, maybe only as a brother, but I'll take it. I'll go back to the base with you; I more than trust you." Then he added, "You're still on the hook for taking a swimming lesson tomorrow, though."

Jeff could hardly contain himself, at least at first. But then, when he replayed some of what Matt had said in his head, he poked back, "Brother? Who said anything about loving you as a brother? I've got four of those already, and that's enough, thank you very much. Come here, I'll show you "brother," and reached to grab Matt, but he wasn't quick enough, Matt had already bolted to the far corner of the room, taking the blanket with him out of modesty.

Thomas Willard © 2021

Jeff got up out of bed, naked, and walked towards Matt. "You think you're safe there because I'm naked, but my brothers didn't respect personal boundaries, so I have no shame, especially not with you. I've learned a few secrets dancing with you, and believe me, you're in big trouble now."

Matt realized he was trapped and had nowhere to run. He figured he'd try to bargain with Jeff, trade a truce for no more swimming lessons, but it was too late. Jeff grabbed the blanket, throwing it to the floor. Now, they were both naked. "We're even again," Jeff said, "just the way I like it." Then he pounced.

What Jeff had discovered while dancing with Matt was that he was ticklish. So, that was his first line of attack. Once Matt was begging him to stop, Jeff taunted him again, asking, "Brothers? Are we still just brothers?"

Finally, Matt surrendered and agreed, saying, "Ok, I give. We're not just brothers."

Jeff, still not satisfied, said, "If we're not brothers, then I want a hug."

Thomas Willard © 2021

Matt, totally exhausted, said, "Fine," and wrapped his arms around Jeff.

That was what Jeff was waiting for because it wasn't just that Matt was ticklish; Jeff had also discovered that Matt became extremely excited when his butt was squeezed, something even Matt didn't know about himself yet. As soon as Matt had put his arms around him, Jeff reached around and grabbed Matt's butt with both hands. The results were immediate. Matt moaned and then tried to escape, but it was already too late. He quickly passed the point of no return, but as he did, he kissed Jeff on the mouth for the first time.

Jeff waited for the afterglow to pass before releasing Matt from the hug. Then, in a self-satisfied tone, said, "Brothers, huh?" Matt just nodded yes in a weak attempt at defiance.

They both crawled back into bed for another nap after Matt had retrieved the blanket from the floor. Jeff dried them both with his discarded t-shirt. As they started to drift off to sleep, Jeff said, "Hey, we're not even anymore. Should I be worried?"

Thomas Willard © 2021

Matt just smiled and said, "Nah. We'll make things even tomorrow in the pool."

As soon as he'd said it, Matt regretted his taunt: he felt that any teasing related to the pool was off-limits. So, quickly, before Jeff had a chance to react to what he'd said, Matt turned to face Jeff, then rolled him onto his back. "I've changed my mind. I think I'll sleep better if things are kept even." Then he laid his head on Jeff's chest and began to stroke him. He'd learned some things about Jeff, too, when they'd danced: Jeff liked attention paid to his neck and ears. So, Matt started nuzzling and lightly kissing the side of Jeff's neck and his ear.

Jeff instantly responded physically and began to moan. "Hey, no fair. you weren't supposed to notice any of my sensitive areas." But Matt just kept up his affectionate assault until, after just a few minutes, and with a loud groan, Jeff erupted three times.

Matt wiped Jeff clean with his towel, then said, "I'm sorry for teasing you about tomorrow. Forgive me?"

Thomas Willard © 2021

Jeff replied with a contented smile, "What answer will get you to do that again?" But when he saw Matt was serious, he stopped teasing and, looking Matt in the eyes, said, "I trust you. I know you'd never deliberately hurt me." Then, he kissed him on the forehead.

Matt wanted Jeff to have a safe place, his back again, the next day when they were in the pool, so he rolled onto his side and pulled Jeff's arm to his chest until they were spooned together.

Jeff said, "This feels good." Then he remembered the image of Matt in the ambulance, ashen, dying from lack of blood.

"I know it sounds stupid, but sometimes I have bad memories. I'll need to hold you like this to convince myself that you're alright."

Matt knew what Jeff meant exactly. Ever since the flight, he'd been having flashbacks of seeing the Germans closing in on Jeff, getting ready to slaughter him. Jeff had just triggered another flashback, and suddenly, Matt needed to hold him.

Thomas Willard © 2021

"I have the same problem. I know it's not rational, but I get frightened, too, sometimes. I'm feeling that way now. Could we switch for just a second?"

Jeff was already rolling over before Matt finished speaking. He grabbed Matt's arm and pulled him in tight. "You never have to ask. Hold me as long as you want; I'm not going anywhere." Then he added, "Looks like we both are haunted by some bad memories, and holding each other is probably the only way to get rid of them.

"It's not stupid to feel this way after what we've both seen, but I think we can help each other get over it.

"We'll make a pact: whoever needs to holds the other for as long as he wants. And just so you know, you can hold me for ten years, and I won't mind.

"We won't keep track of whose turn it is or try to keep things even. And I promise, no teasing ever, not about this."

Matt held Jeff for about ten minutes until the panic feeling had passed, and then he reversed positions with him again. He wanted Jeff to sleep in that position next to him, secure, holding him close from the back. He hoped this would make Jeff feel safe and protected the next day in the pool.

#

WINGMEN

For the rest of the week, Matt and Jeff followed a loose schedule of swimming lessons in the morning for Jeff and dancing lessons in the early afternoon for Matt. Sometimes, when the weather was nice, they'd delay their return from the YMCA and explore the countryside on their loaner bicycles.

Both had made quick progress. Jeff had first learned to float, then how to swim using the breaststroke, and finally, using the front crawl. By Thursday, he was swimming the length of the pool, no longer concerned whether he was in the deep end or not.

Matt was well past any shyness with Jeff and discovered he loved dancing, especially with Jeff. They always practiced in just their t-shirt and boxers – anything less and neither one could focus – and by Thursday, they'd progressed to a few fast songs. No matter what, they always finished with the slow song, "It's Been A Long Time." They couldn't practice that song enough.

They were at the pool, early as usual, on Friday morning when Captain Spiegel, in uniform, appeared. He'd managed to get away from the hospital for a few hours and thought he'd come to see how his two favorite fighter pilots were doing.

Matt got out of the pool first and greeted the Captain with a hug, soaking him in the process. He started to apologize for giving him a hard time in the interview, but the Captain stopped him. By then, Jeff had joined them. Jeff shook the Captain's hand, then turned to Matt and said, "Just tell him thanks, Matt."

With tears streaming down his face, Matt said, "Thank you so much. You've saved my life. I'll never forget what you did." Then he hugged the Captain again, getting him even wetter. Jeff figured the Captain was already wet, so he gave him a hug, too.

Captain Spiegel had managed to borrow a camera and asked if he could take a picture of them both swimming in the

Thomas Willard © 2021

pool. He was headed back to the States and would send a copy to each of their families.

They both jumped in the pool and pretended to race for a lap, Matt letting Jeff win. But they had been working on something else, and Matt asked if the Captain would take a picture of Jeff doing it.

They got out of the water and walked to the deep end of the pool. Matt nodded encouragement, and Jeff walked out to the end of the diving board. He first looked at Matt and then at Captain Spiegel and asked if he was all set. The Captain asked Jeff to wait for a second so he could find the best spot to take the picture from and focus the camera. Then he said he was ready, and Jeff dove head-first into the water.

Captain Spiegel had positioned himself so that both Matt and Jeff were in the frame. The picture he captured was of a fearless, determined Jeff in the foreground, just before he entered the water, and of a proud Matt in the background going absolutely berserk.

Thomas Willard © 2021

Captain Spiegel chatted with the manager while he waited for Matt and Jeff to change. They loaded the bikes in the back of the car, and all three squeezed into the front seat for the short drive back to the Manor.

Once there, Jeff asked Captain Spiegel if he would take a picture of Matt dancing. The Captain said that was a great idea. Jeff asked one of the Red Cross women if she would dance with Matt, and before a less-than-confident Matt could think of an excuse, Jeff had selected a song and set up the record player. "Matt, this is the one we practiced yesterday; you did great. I know you've got this. If not, I promise that camera will have seen better days." Then Jeff pushed play.

The latest Mills Brother's hit, "Paper Doll," began with a slow, gentle rhythm. Matt and the Red Cross woman danced a slow dance style, but halfway through, the song switched to an upbeat tempo, and the couple changed to swing dance.

The song lasted for about two and a half minutes, with Captain Spiegel taking a total of ten pictures from as many positions. He managed to capture the picture he wanted: of a smiling, relaxed Matt and the Red Cross woman in the foreground and a wildly clapping-to-the-music, encouraging Jeff in the background.

All three men thanked the Red Cross woman, who kissed Matt on the cheek, breaking all the rules against it, before going into the small visiting psychiatrist's office together.

Captain Spiegel closed the door and said he'd have to leave in a minute but that he just wanted to say something first. As always, he got right to the point.

"Love sometimes comes from bonding over a shared experience. Your shared experience is off the charts, even for fighter pilots. So, I've turned the question around from how could you have bonded so closely to how could you not have, given your incredible common experience?

"Matt, before you think I'm hinting at gratitude, I'm not. Under the extreme stress of combat, Jeff got to know you as he would never have otherwise, like no one has known you before or is likely to ever again. He started by admiring you, your character, but eventually, that admiration grew into love and caring, surprising himself but not frightening him.

"I seriously doubt that he'll ever have these feelings for another male, but he has them for you in spades, and because they are based on a bedrock-solid view and appreciation of your character, they are not going to fade with time. If anything, they'll only grow stronger. And, from someone who's gotten to know you a little, Matt, I don't blame him.

"As far as your feelings for Jeff go, they may have started out as a crush, admiration for his flying and dancing skills, and his easy, friendly way with people. But you noticed other things: when he went out of his way to befriend you when others didn't even see you, how he could be gentle when someone like you needed it, and just his overall empathy towards you and others. Your admiration also turned into love and caring, and since the flight, it has grown without bound as he continues to reinforce your view of him, by what he did to save you after the flight and what he does every day to show you how much he cares for you.

"I think love is gender-blind, and except for societal pressure, it is not naturally restrained to stay within current social-norm physical limits; you give yourself, body and soul, as much as you can, to provide whatever the person you love needs.

"Matt, Jeff knew you were terrified of being physically intimate with him, so he risked everything and violated his own personal code of ethics to force himself on you – I take some blame for encouraging him - in a desperate gamble that your terror was based on shyness, inexperience, and doubt that he could possibly want you that way, and not from a lack of interest in him by you. He's fearless, a force of nature when it comes to you. No wonder you love him so much; I've gotten to know him, too, and I'm more than a little envious of you.

"The only ones that will understand your closeness will be other fighter pilots. If later any ask you about it, tell them you were fighter pilots in England during WWII and each other's wingman –

Thomas Willard © 2021

I love that term, by the way. They'll see you as a single entity, as I do, and not question how close you are and might even be a little envious, too. No one else could possibly understand – I've tried, and only can a little - so ignore them; their opinion doesn't count.

"Psychiatry is in its infancy, and a lot of its teachings are just outright wrong, especially when it comes to same-gender relationships. Today's practice of trying to eliminate male-male bonds judged to be too close is ineffectual at best - since it goes against human nature, it's bound to fail - or is downright harmful and cruel. Sometime in the future, it'll be harshly viewed as barbaric and unethical. I hope someday I can contribute to bringing that change about. But that won't help you two now or in the foreseeable future.

"Just know that change will come and that you are not alone. There are others, surprisingly close to you, that share your problem, and even more that support change and will gladly turn a blind eye in order to protect you.

Thomas Willard © 2021

"The official Army position is that those in male-male relationships should be rooted out and discharged. But unofficially, I've found commanders, especially Air Force commanders, very sympathetic and tolerant since they know how much you rely on each other every day to survive. Who are they to decide where the closeness line should be drawn? Anytime I've been called in to evaluate a male bonding issue, the entire chain of command has accepted my conclusion that there was no issue, then quietly asked me to give the two men involved some tips on being more discreet.

"I haven't shared any details of your relationship with anyone and won't. Nothing has been documented. I'll provide my evaluation results to Doctor Garnett verbally, by phone, that you both show no signs of combat fatigue, and recommend you should be allowed to return to duty. But, per my confidentiality agreement with him, I will not share any details.

"Doctor Garnett already suspects you two have bonded, though, or he wouldn't have sought me, a recognized heretic, out. He cares about you both a lot and has your back. My guess is he'll make some arrangements, starting with housing, that will give you some privacy. If you ever need help, I think you can safely go to him, but keep things vague: provide just enough detail so that he understands the issue, but not enough that you place him in a conflicted, divided-loyalty position between you and the Army.

"I'll always be available to help in any way that I can. They're sending me back to the States soon, but I'll leave my contact information with Doctor Garnett, and he will be able to reach me. When this war is over, I've been offered a faculty position at Brandeis University in the Boston area, and you should be able to reach me there. No worries about me forgetting who you are: I'll remember you two for the rest of my life."

Captain Spiegel hugged each of them before opening the door. Then, he shook each of their hands in the foyer before leaving. At the time Captain Spiegel helped Matt and Jeff, he was 33 years old.

Neither Matt nor Jeff would ever meet Captain Spiegel face-to-face again, though a desperate Matt would reach out to him by phone eight years later.

****

After the war and his discharge from the US Army Medical Corps, Dr. John Paul Spiegel joined the faculty of Brandeis University in Waltham, Massachusetts. There, he became an expert on urban violence and, from 1966 to 1979, headed the Lemberg Center of the Study of Violence.

In 1973, he became President of the American Psychiatric Association (APA). As president-elect, he helped to change the definition of homosexuality in the Diagnostic and Statistical Manual of Mental Disorders (DSM), where homosexuality had previously been described as sexual deviance and homosexuals as pathological.

After 1973, the official position of the APA became homosexuality was no longer considered a disease but a natural human condition. The previous treatments to change a person's sexual preference - through drugs, psychoanalysis, or shock therapy – were considered unethical. The only approved treatment was to help a person accept and feel comfortable with his sexuality and to repair any damage society or religion may have done.

This fundamental change in how homosexuals are perceived by the APA started the dramatic shift in how society as a whole views homosexuals and resulted in profound changes in society, in equal rights laws, and, most importantly, in how homosexuals view themselves. Homosexuals the world over owe this now mostly forgotten man - and all his progressive, compassionate colleagues in the APA in 1973 - an enormous debt of gratitude.

CHAPTER 5 — WORMINGFORD AIRFIELD: RETURN TO DUTY: END OF APRIL 1944

WELCOME BACK

At the end of April, Matt and Jeff returned to duty and discovered two major changes, purposely kept from them by Doctor Garnett and Captain Spiegel to preserve their stress-free stay at the Manor, had occurred with the Group.

The first, most significant change was that they had a new Commanding Officer, Colonel George Crowell: Colonel Jenkins had been shot down two weeks earlier, leading an airdrome strafing mission in France. He'd survived the crash but was now a POW.

The second change was the Group had moved to a new airfield, Wormingford Airfield, USAAF Station 159, in the county of Colchester, about 32 miles east of Nuthampstead and 50 miles northwest of London. The move was made to reduce the distance the fighters had to fly to reach the Channel and to vacate Nuthampstead for the bomber group it had been built for, the 398th Bombardment Group, flying B-17s and newly arrived from the States.

Doctor Garnett had instructed the driver sent to retrieve Matt and Jeff from the Manor to deliver them to his office. There, he'd welcomed them back, briefed them on the changes, and said they were to report to Colonel Crowell after their meeting with him but had a few things he needed to discuss with them first.

He said he knew how much they'd admired Colonel Jenkins, how much he'd meant to them. But then he told them Colonel Crowell was just like Colonel Jenkins - he led from the front and was extremely concerned for the welfare of his men - and that they should think of Colonel Crowell as a two-month younger version of Colonel Jenkins.

Colonel Jenkins had shared all that he knew about the rescue flight and the post-flight with Colonel Crowell, and they had come to the same conclusion: that both Matt and Jeff should be submitted for the Congressional Medal of Honor but would respect their wishes not to be. Both Colonels had taken some heat from the higher-ups but had held firm.

Doctor Garnett then said he had a problem and hoped they could help. Since the move, and with a large influx of new pilots, he realized the need for a Group-level transient barracks to house newly-arrived pilots - before they were assigned to a squadron and permanent barracks - and for temporary visitors. And he thought that having permanent-resident mentors living in the barracks – experienced pilots, but only slightly higher in rank, available to offer guidance - would help the new pilots transition. He mentioned the idea to Colonel Crowell, who liked it very much.

Thomas Willard © 2021

He was hoping Matt and Jeff would be willing to act as mentors. The barracks held up to 20 pilots but would rarely be full, even sometimes empty. And to offer a little more privacy with all the turnover, a two-man room was walled off to house the mentors, with a door that closed.

Matt and Jeff said they'd be glad to be mentors and then thanked the Doctor, shaking his hand. Doctor Garnett said he'd hoped that they would agree, so he had taken a chance and had their personal belongings from Nuthampstead sent to the transient barracks. He also told them they should reach out to him if they ever had a problem and that he was always available to help before releasing them to report to Colonel Crowell.

Colonel Crowell's office was just a few doors down from Doctor Garnett's. When they were ushered into the Colonel's office by his sergeant-receptionist, they began the normal snap-to-attention-salute to report, but the Colonel, who'd been waiting for them, was too quick and had already reached them and extended his hand.

He welcomed them and said he was very glad to see them back. He shared with them his grief over the loss of Colonel Jenkins: they'd been close friends, and he was going to - was already - missing him a lot. But the sooner they finished the war, the sooner Colonel Jenkins would be free.

He told them they were arriving just in time; the Group was about to get very busy. Everyone knew there was an imminent Allied invasion planned, though not many knew where or when. Before the invasion could occur, the Allies needed to achieve air superiority over the Germans. But the planners wanted more than superiority; they wanted dominance.

They wanted the Luftwaffe decimated, unable to attack Allied troop transports or landing craft. They wanted the Luftwaffe so reduced in strength that no enemy aircraft would dare enter the skies anywhere near the landing zones or risk immediate annihilation. And they wanted this without reducing fighter-escort support for the bombers.

To quickly meet these objectives, without waging a long war of attrition or needlessly sacrificing his pilots, Colonel Crowell wanted his pilots to only engage enemy fighters when the odds were clearly in their favor: no evenly matched dog fights. This applied only to aerial combat away from the bombers; he still expected fighter escorts to aggressively defend the bombers.

He wanted them to take maximum advantage of the P-38's strengths, like superior concentrated fire-power head-on from a distance and its ability to dive steeply at high speed, to jump enemy fighters from a height, and now, with a growing numerical advantage: Allied fighters already outnumbered the Germans, especially in occupied France and Belgium.

And, he wanted his pilots to not engage and to break engagement if attacked if the odds were even or in favor of the enemy fighter; to live to fight another day, a luxury the German pilots could no longer afford. Like it or not, Matt and Jeff were legends in the P-38 community, and the Colonel wanted them to lead by example, especially for the newer, less experienced pilots.

Thomas Willard © 2021

With Matt and Jeff, the Group was at full strength: 126 pilots. And there were 50% more planes than pilots, so mechanical issues should be quickly dealt with. But a lot of the pilots were new replacements. Colonel Crowell needed flight leaders who could also substitute as mission squadron leaders so pilot mission rotation could be more balanced. He was relying on Matt and Jeff to help fill those roles.

The Colonel was aware of some of the details of the rescue flight and the post-flight. Every aspect of it astounded him, and he had enormous respect for them both. He did have one concern: that in combat, with one of them under attack, the other might show a reckless disregard for his own life to try to save him. This would be bad enough if he was on his own, but if he was leading a flight or squadron, that could mean disaster. They were both held in such high esteem by the other pilots in the squadron that they'd all follow them.

Colonel Crowell said, though, that when he'd discussed his concern with Doctor Garnett, who'd had the same worry and discussed it previously with Captain Spiegel, the three of them had independently come to the same conclusion.

Matt and Jeff were too responsible to ever put others or the mission at risk. The problem would come after the mission when one of them didn't return. If that happened, the other should immediately be grounded.

But to reduce the stress on them, their two doctors had made a few recommendations for mission assignments. They should be assigned to the same missions if possible: that would reduce their worrying about one another when they should be relaxing between missions. And they should lead or be part of different flights, unless for smaller missions where they weren't needed to lead and could be each other's wingman: then it would be their job to protect each other.

Matt and Jeff said that all made perfect sense and were relieved that the doctors had considered how they might react in combat when the other was threatened: they'd worried about that themselves. Colonel Crowell said he was implementing all the doctor's recommendations, so he had no concerns, and any pilot who did might find himself in a Flak House for a week or two of forced rest. Then he saluted them before dismissing them.

Matt and Jeff asked the sergeant-receptionist for directions to the transient barracks and found it was just a short walk from where they were: Group Headquarters.

When they arrived, they found the barracks empty and walked to the rear, where their walled-off quarters were. All their belongings had safely made the trip from Nuthampstead and been hung in lockers with their names on them.

When they tried closing the door, they discovered the door had been installed so that the door could only be locked and unlocked from the inside.

THE END

Thomas Willard © 2021

Thank you for taking the time to read "Lightning Wingman." Please take a moment to rate and review the book; your interest and feedback are greatly appreciated.

The story continues with "Mustang Wingman," book #2 in the Wingman series, available on Amazon at

https://www.amazon.com/dp/B09RVN16WW

Thomas Willard © 2021

www.ingramcontent.com/pod-product-compliance
Lightning Source LLC
LaVergne TN
LVHW040250121224
798954LV00026B/228